# Lucía Ashta

# SIX SHOOTER
## AND A SHIFTER

## WHEN THE MOON SHINES

# When the Moon Shines

# When the Moon Shines

## BOOK ONE IN THE SIX SHOOTER AND A SHIFTER SERIES

LUCÍA ASHTA

When the Moon Shines

Book One in the Six Shooter and a Shifter series

Copyright © 2022 by Lucía Ashta

www.LuciaAshta.com

All rights reserved. No part of this book may be reproduced in any form or by any electronic or mechanical means, including information storage and retrieval systems, without written permission from the author, except for the use of brief quotations in a book review.

This is a work of fiction. Any resemblance to actual persons, places, or events is purely coincidental.

Cover design by Mirela Barbu

Editing by Ocean's Edge Editing

Proofreading by Geesey Editorial Services

*For the unexpected twists and turns that make life such a thrilling surprise. Sometimes it turns out best when we don't get what we think we want.*

♥

*And for my daughters and beloved. Always. You make every day so much better.*

A good horse is more important than a good man, but if you can have both, do that.

— LORETTA MAYBELLE RAY ~
SHERIFF OF TRAITOR'S DEN

# When the Moon Shines

## CHAPTER 1
## *Keep Your Cock Problems to Yourself*

Without waiting for me to catch up, Tiger ducked under the swinging doors of the saloon, whined when his fur caught, then settled on the floor next to my usual table in the back.

I scowled at him over the doors while removing the tuft of orange fur. Pocketing the puffy strands so Sharmayne wouldn't holler at me for dirtying her floor, I pushed through and crossed the room to pull out the chair next to Tiger's sizable bulk.

"Howdy there, Loretta," Sharmayne called, already sashaying in my direction. "Saw Tiger come in, knew you'd be right behind the good for nothin'. Isn't that right, boy?"

Sharmayne was voluptuous, bordering on voluminous, but her ample curves were in all the right places, straining the integrity of her patterned dress. She crouched next to Tiger, scratching behind his ears while she slid a bowl of water in front of him.

He began to lap it up, making both too much noise and too much mess, splashing water onto the floor's worn wooden planks.

"Now that's a good boy," Sharmayne cooed, even though Tiger hadn't done anything particularly good. If I were the one to slop water all over her floor, I'd be hearing about it from now till next Sunday.

"You do remember he's not a *boy*, but a shifter *man* trapped in his tiger form, right?" I asked, though this certainly wasn't news.

"Such a good boy," she went on, giving him a full head rub, all while ignoring me.

I'd take offense if not for the fact that Sharmayne liked animals more than she liked most people.

"Just making sure," I muttered, pushing out the chair next to me and kicking up my dusty boots ... which put them at eye level for Sharmayne.

She squinted at my shoes and started to rise to her full height, which wouldn't have been particularly impressive if not for the fact that I was sitting and now peering up at her. "Loretta Maybelle Ray..."

I sighed loudly and obnoxiously. Nothing good ever followed the use of my full name.

"I know you don't go puttin' your feet up on your momma's furniture when you're in her house. Collette would tan your hide."

While a blatant exaggeration since my momma did as much doting as she did scolding, Sharmayne did have a point.

Another sigh. "Stop busting my balls, Shar. It's been a long day and I just want to kick back with one of your amazing drinks. You know how much I love them."

Sharmayne tsked at me, but I could tell my compliment had done its job. She pulled a rag from her dainty apron and wiped down the already clean table.

"If I was to be bustin' your lady balls, Loretta, you'd know it. Trust me on that."

I definitely did. Sharmayne's talent for ball busting was well known all across town, which, given the size of the place, wasn't saying all that much.

Even so, the small town was all I'd ever known. All I'd ever know, unless Uncle Tucker decided to show up to let us all out already.

Sharmayne straightened. "The usual, honey?"

*See?* Compliments always pay off...

"Yes, ma'am. Thank you kindly."

Giving me an approving nod, Sharmayne bustled back to her bar.

"You don't help things by being so friendly," I mumbled to Tiger, who continued to lap up water in the most obnoxious way possible.

I registered what I said and chuckled to find myself talking to my constant animal companion—yet again—drawing looks from the handful of other patrons in Sharmayne's Den. The sun was still up, so the establishment was mostly empty. It'd be hopping in a few hours.

I felt Sharmayne returning before I saw her crossing the room back toward me. The heat of her stare on my boots reached through the beat-up leather to tingle the skin of my feet.

Rolling my eyes in a way she wouldn't see, I plastered a smile on my face and swung my legs down off the chair a moment before she slid a Moon Mixer across the smooth table at me.

I caught it, holding the mug of swirling, milky white liquid in both hands, enjoying the cold of it against my palms.

"Mmm-mmm." This time, I wasn't even trying to blow smoke up her skirt. "I've been dreaming of having one of these since Leroy and Ollie walked into my office."

Sharmayne frowned and shook her head, her chignon holding strong; not a single strand of her brown hair tumbled loose. It wouldn't dare.

"Those men only got one oar in the water between the two of 'em. What were they goin' on about this time?"

"Oh, apparently Leroy's rooster keeps escaping his pen to harass Ollie's hens. Ollie's complaining that the cock's causing fights among the ladies since they all want to have at him first." I snickered at the memory of having to keep a straight face while the neighbors yelled at each other, saying *cock* this and *cock* that.

"And the fools can't figure that one out on their own without involving the sheriff? Don't they realize you got better things to do?" Again, Sharmayne shook her head. "They could throw themselves at the ground and still miss."

"Tell me about it." I held up a finger and thumb, almost touching. "I'm this close to ordering them to move away from each other. That's why I've been sorely needing one of these." I lifted my Moon Mixer in front of my face.

Sharmayne patted the table. "Sounds like you've

earned it good and well. Enjoy, honey, and let me know when you're ready for another."

Smiling my thanks, I pulled in my first sip slowly, savoring the sweetly tart taste. I'd never bothered to ask exactly what was in it. Sharmayne liked to keep her secrets, and I liked to keep on good terms with her. She ran the only reputable saloon in town and wielded her power to ban any patrons like a lethal weapon. No one wanted to be forbidden from hanging out in the most popular joint around.

The Moon Mixer tasted like candy, got me tipsy —or drunk when I overindulged—and was mesmerizing to watch. Smoky tendrils of white that mimicked moonlight swam around the glass until the last drop was drained.

A witch with low-grade powers, Sharmayne went for show, adding a small spell to her entire list of drinks. Her liquid offerings were so spectacular that no one ever complained about how poor the food was.

With Sharmayne busying herself once more behind the bar, I surreptitiously kicked my legs back up, slumped in my chair, and nursed my drink. I was usually on duty until sundown, but as sheriff I was giving myself the authority to call it a day. The mayor was unlikely to notice, since he spent most of his workday bent over a golf club—or a woman who wasn't his wife.

Besides, anyone would need a stiff drink after dealing with Leroy and Ollie for the full hour I had. They'd been coming to see me with equally frivolous complaints nearly twice a month. Something had to give.

Placing my Stetson on the table, I shook out my dark hair, letting my scalp breathe. The day was hot, though not scorching. Those days would come soon enough though.

Without wanting to, my thoughts wandered back to the two men who used to be best friends before they had a bitter falling out over a woman. The story was a lasting theme around these parts. Neither Leroy nor Ollie ended up with Letitia, but their rivalry endured, making their neighboring homesteads sworn enemies.

Maybe I could convince one of the mages in town to do a spell on them? The residents frowned upon using magic on each other, but desperate times called for desperate measures. Not many folks around these parts were sticklers for the rules. If one of the witches or wizards gave me a good deal on their services, I was going to consider it. Mayor Reginald Roone would think twice before admonishing me, especially when I knew his secrets. Everyone in town seemed to know about his adultery—all but his wife.

She, Magnolia Roone, was as sweet as my drink, and I'd come perilously close to warning her about her husband's true nature more times than I could count. But there was no escaping our small town, and I had to work with her husband. In theory, he was my boss, even if he didn't act like it. With regret, I'd kept my mouth shut every time, hoping someone else would alert the kind woman to the weasel who shared her bed.

I took another sip of my drink and studied the saloon. Buster Brane, whose name didn't reference his level of moderate intelligence, was sporting droopy eyelids and a number of empty mugs on his table. Since he'd caught his wife cheating on him—with the mayor—he'd become a day drinker.

If I hadn't had such an annoying day already, I would've joined him. Tried to pep him up a little. He was a nice enough guy when he wasn't crying into his drink.

Next was Henrietta Hammer. She was an odd one to find here while it was still light out...

After convincing myself that my job entailed keeping tabs on all the residents, whether I was on duty or not, I was halfway out of my seat to go speak with her when the bell rang.

And not just any bell, *the* bell.

"Aw, hot damn. This day just keeps getting better and bloody better." I downed half my drink without a look of appreciation at the mesmerizing moonlight inside my mug.

"Don't ya hear that, Loretta?" Sharmayne called from across the saloon—as if there were a chance in blazing hell I could miss the clanging; it was loud enough to rouse the newly dead. Thankfully, so far we'd only had two residents die, and none had walked out of their graves yet. Given the varied citizenry of Traitor's Den, there was no telling what might happen with enough time, however.

"Loretta..." Sharmayne repeated.

"Yeah, yeah. I hear it all right." I drained the rest of my drink. What a shame to have to hurry it up, but I wasn't about to waste a drop, if for no other reason than I might offend Sharmayne. We regulars of her saloon directed an unreasonable amount of thought to making sure we didn't upset the matron, who was loose with the alcohol—and her snap judgments.

When I dragged my chair back along the floor as

if it were leaden, Tiger looked up at me, big ears perked. Everything about him was large.

"Sorry, buddy. But we gotta go."

He whimpered.

"I know. I'm feeling ya hard right now, but you know how it is. I'm the sheriff. I put my life on the line for the good people of Traitor's Den every single day."

Tiger was polite enough to ignore my double set of exaggerations. Despite its rowdy and varied population, my life had never been truly in danger.

I didn't go anywhere without my matching set of six shooters and I wasn't afraid to use them when people got to misbehaving. One was loaded with regular bullets, the other with silver.

The residents of Traitor's Den weren't all good. Some were fair to poor on the quality-people meter. But they were damn entertaining after a few Moon Mixers, I'd give them that.

With Tiger at my side and my hat back on my head where it belonged, I was almost at the swinging doors when they snapped open inward, slamming against both sides of the wall from the force.

"Dammit, Hank Henry," Sharmayne snarled. "How many times do I gotta tell you to take it easy on my doors? You break 'em, I'm gonna make ya fix 'em, ya hear me?"

"Loud and clear, ma'am," Hank Henry said, because Hank was smart enough to know when to back down from an enraged saloon owner. But his gaze zeroed in on me immediately after.

"Ya'd better hurry. Two guys just came through the portal and they're fightin' up a storm."

I rushed out, knowing that Sharmayne would add my Moon Mixer to my tab like she always did. Buster, Henrietta, and the last two patrons of the bar ran out behind me.

We hadn't had a newcomer in nearly a year, so long that I worried the pocket portal might have closed entirely from the other side. And we'd never had anyone come through fighting. The whole town was going to turn out for the show.

The portal was at the far edge of town, so I ran for my horse, who waited for me just outside. Jolene was a stunning Appaloosa with lots of brown spots, a caramel-colored mane, a large white patch across her face, and bright blue eyes. Without using the stirrups, I grabbed on to the horn of the saddle, pushed off the ball of my left foot, and leapt into the seat.

"How long ago'd they come through?" I asked

Hank, wrapping my fingers around the reins, itching to take off.

"Maybe five minutes ago? Maybe more. I only just heard the relay signal and ran to ring the bell. Then I came to find you."

Without another word to him or anyone, I clicked my tongue at Jolene, and the mare charged forward, Tiger at our side.

## CHAPTER 2
## *Motherflapping Flashers and Other Rules to Break*

The stampeding hooves of other horses thundered behind us, but I didn't turn to look. Neither did Tiger. There weren't many options when it came to who might be following us, and we knew them all by name.

The residents of Traitor's Den were a lot of things, most of them colorful, but they were one and all nosy as nosy got.

They were the only ones who could be racing at our backs, aiming to reach the portal before it vanished. We'd never managed to catch it open—not once in twenty-three years—but there was a first time for everything, and we were a relentlessly hopeful bunch.

Loping beside Jolene, Tiger yipped a warning.

"You heard him, Jo," I shouted over the rumbling of her hooves. "Give it all you got, girl."

It was cheeky of me to spur her onward when she was already galloping at full tilt, but I was also seeing what Tiger had reacted to.

The bright, nearly blinding lights of the portal, the color of lightning, were sputtering as they reached toward each other to shut.

Jolene lurched, stretching even her neck forward.

*Damn. We might just make it,* I thought, unwilling to voice the hope aloud. I didn't want to let either of my friends down, and Tiger and Jolene were some of the best friends a girl could ask for.

"Yeehaw," someone called from behind, and from the sound of it, I guessed it was Hank Henry. He'd taken to the Western theme of the town better than a duck to water. I had no idea what he'd been like before the portal spit him out here, but now he was all clanking spurs and bow-legged swagger.

"Woo, woo, whooooop," followed next, and I'd still bet on Hank. If he had a fault, it was over-enthusiasm, and who could blame a guy for making the best of a crappy deal?

A glance to my side revealed that his horse, Chester Bo, was about to pass us. The stallion was a fine specimen, all sleek muscle, a winning attitude, and more speed than Hank Henry could usually handle.

Jolene wasn't about to let him beat her. She pulled on reserves I didn't know she had and launched us back solidly in the lead as we sailed up to Portal Platform, where Jolene hit the brakes and skidded to a stop, nearly throwing me. Clamping my calves so tightly around her sides that I worried I'd hurt her, and lowering my torso over her back while I held on to the horn of the saddle with everything I had, I managed to keep my seat.

The second I was certain I wouldn't fall, I swung my leg over and slid down her side, not bothering to tie her up to one of the many hitching posts installed for that purpose. Jolene was as loyal as a good, faithful dog—and far easier to ride. She wasn't going anywhere without me. Besides, she was as nosy as the townies, and there was little better than first-hand observation, even for a horse.

Tiger at my side while Jolene remained behind, her sides heaving as she caught her breath, chuffing and snorting, which I interpreted as her cheering us on, we ran toward the rapidly shrinking portal, bypassing two brawling men—one had the other pulled into a headlock that didn't look like it was going to hold.

As sheriff, they'd become my problem soon enough. For now, I had bigger fish to fry.

I jumped up onto Portal Platform—Mayor Roone's fancy name for a rickety wooden scaffold a couple of feet off the hard-packed dirt that occupied the space immediately below the portal, which hovered around four feet up. The bed-sized platform cut the fall when the portal shot anyone out to a comfortable *oomph* and a couple of passing bruises.

The gateway usually stretched open around ten feet. It was currently half as wide, diminishing in size, sparking like the worst of fire hazards.

Even so, Bobbie Sue and Ashton Blu were there, crouched to either side of the portal, exchanging a loaded look. They didn't say anything to me, or even acknowledge me, and I understood why.

This was the opportunity we'd been anticipating for more than eleven long months, since the last time it opened. And time was ticking away as they gathered the gumption to do what they'd been planning for just as long.

"Go, Ashton Blu," I said in a quick rush, tone full of pep.

With his snout, Tiger nudged the cowboy with the unruly hair and button nose on the shoulder.

"Whatcha waitin' for?" I asked.

He swallowed, his Adam's apple bobbing beneath three-day-old scruff.

Bobbie Sue handed me a glass bottle with a piece of paper rolled inside it. "If he's got cold feet, I'll go, then. You toss this in as soon as I'm clear," she told me and stood.

Tiger whined; I grimaced. "It's shrinking fast. It's now or never, guys." When neither hastened to jump through the portal, I added, "I'll do it, then."

I turned to Tiger. "You stay and take care of Jolene."

The tip of one of my boots was caressing the shimmering light stretching between the sparking circle, when Ashton Blu tugged me back.

Without another word, he ran at the portal and jumped through.

My eyes grew wide and I turned to stare at Bobbie Sue. Her eyes were just as big as she grabbed the bottle from me and tossed it through.

Thirty seconds later, the portal was a flat circle the size of a watermelon. Twenty seconds after, it sucked fully to a close with a slurping *shloooop*.

The portal vanished entirely ... taking Ashton Blu with it.

"Holy bald bluebells," Bobbie Sue whispered. "It finally worked. After all this time..." She shook her head in awe, large, floppy red curls bouncing. "Well, that just dills my pickle. I can't believe it finally hap—"

Bobbie Sue froze. I froze. Even Tiger stilled for several seconds as the sputtering that indicated a portal started popping in the empty air around us.

From the large, equally rickety viewing stand behind and above us, Jim Bob One—not to be confused with Jim Bob Two—leaned out from the open window. "What's going on, y'all? Sounds like another one's opening. But that can't be. It's—"

A long, trailing screech cut him off, and he took off his Stetson to scratch at what was left of his hair. "Why's a woman screamin'? I don't see no woman."

Neither did I. But he was right, it did sound like a woman was screaming. Somewhere. Though I doubted that's what it actually was.

We were in the middle of wide open, dry, dusty desert, as far as the eye could see. Even beyond the boundary that none of us could cross, it was still sunbaked earth. Its reddish hue seemed to glow as the sun steadily made its way toward the flat horizon.

I inched to the edge of Portal Platform, searching on all sides of us. "Well ... I got no idea what's goin' on."

The shrieking grew louder, stretching out into a

wail as the portal sprang back to life, singeing my nose hairs before I managed to whip my face out of the way.

Rubbing at my nose, I scrunched it, fully ignoring the grunting continuing behind us. From the sound of things, the two men the portal spit out were still going at it.

The portal widened, and Bobbie Sue, Tiger, and I backed out of the way. Up close, the lights were so bright as they whipped into a frenzied circle that I had to squint.

The whine sounded so close and was so high-pitched that Bobbie Sue instinctively leaned toward it, putting her right in front of the portal.

"Back up, Bobbie Sue," I barked at her, but she appeared mesmerized, mouth open, waiting for whatever was about to happen.

And it was clear something was. The portal was now several feet wide.

I dove at her, taking her down to the wooden planks a split second before Ashton Blu shot back out of the portal like a ball from a cannon. His arms outstretched, he landed on Portal Platform with a pained grunt, bounced once, twice, from the force with which he was ejected, then rolled off the side, landing in a heap with another grunt.

"Uggggh," he groaned, and as if that wasn't enough to get his point across, "Owwwww."

The portal narrowed behind us until it was no wider than my arm, shot the blue bottle back out of it, then seemed to pause.

The bottle hit the platform hard enough to dent the wood, flipped, hit again, leaving another scuff, then rolled ... and fell off the stand and unerringly bonked Ashton Blu on the head.

"Ouuuuuuch."

As if satisfied its projectile had hit the mark, the portal whipped shut with another loud *shloooooop*.

Despite the afterimages dancing across my vision, I stared at Bobbie Sue. She stared back for a long beat until I shook off my shock and raced to Ashton Blu.

Tiger jumped off the platform and started licking at the hand covering Ashton's bare head until the man moved it. Tiger's long sloppy tongue tried to soothe his pain as his head swelled into a lump, the bottle appearing innocent at his feet, the note still inside it.

That's when I realized his head was—

"Aww, what in all tarnation!" Ashton Blu rumbled. "The portal stole my hat."

Yep. It sure had.

"That was my favorite hat."

As far as I knew, that was also Ashton Blu's only hat. I still felt his pain. A cowboy without his lucky hat was like a cock without his feathers.

"What's goin' on down there?" Jim Bob One called in his hoarse voice, like grit on sandpaper. "Don't make me come down there," he warned, making me wonder whom exactly he was addressing, and if he realized he couldn't exactly discipline a portal. Especially not one that blatantly disregarded our wishes, no matter how many times we called on it to open at our command.

"Loretta Maybelle," Buster Brane called out. "It's lookin' like we need our sheriff over here. Make quick of it."

Sure enough, the two men were still locked in each other's grips, rolling around on the ground, gathering dust as they went like it was in style.

Scowling at the imbeciles—as if we needed any more of those in this town—I hopped down from the stand and stalked over to them, Tiger back at my side, all done nursing Ashton Blu's wounds now that trouble was brewing.

"That's enough, you two," I said in that steady, strong voice I used when I needed to inspire respect.

It worked better than the shiny brass badge I wore looped through my belt.

With most people anyhow...

The two men didn't even pause.

I reached down to grab one of them by the back of the neck. "I said, *That's enough*."

While the one had stopped when I gripped him, the second one just jerked the man away from me, rolling on top of him to pummel him in the face.

Huffing, I frowned and slid Big Bertha from her holster. I popped the cylinder open and let the bullets fall into my open palm. Then I loaded blanks from my belt, spinning the cylinder closed with a click, and pointed Big Bertha skyward and shot.

Bam. Bam. Bam. Bam.

Not a single resident of Traitor's Den flinched, nor did a horse spook; they were all trained not to react to gunshots since they were part of daily life.

But the two new men sure startled.

They separated and jumped to their feet, crouching into low squats.

At least they had decent reflexes. Those would serve them well here where the unlikely seemed to happen when it was least expected.

I watched them while I loaded my regular lead bullets back into Big Bertha, though I wasn't about to waste good bullets on these two buffoons. Saxon Silver was the only dwarf in town. Since his love of metals was a real thing, he'd claimed the title of blacksmith, which meant he was our only producer of bullets—lead, silver, or otherwise—and he was a stingy puss. No one in Traitor's Den used a bullet when they could shoot empty.

Tucking Big Bertha back where she belonged, I patted both hips—and therefore also both six shooters—and towered over our newest residents.

Both men looked up at my face, then trailed down my body, before tracing the length of my bare legs back up until they tucked into my jean shorts. I usually wore pants for the saddle, but I hadn't been planning on going far today, and it was hotter than the sun's balls even though it wasn't yet summer.

"I'm up here, ya know."

The man with the pitch-dark hair whipped his eyes to my face, appearing repentant.

The other man, however, the one with the shabby blond hair that swept into eyes as bright as the leaves on a willow tree in spring, meandered past my bare stomach—because *hot as balls*—lingered on my cleavage, then my lips, before finally meeting my eyes.

The man was trouble with a capital T.

"Why, hello there," he said in a voice as smooth as churned butter. "What's your name?"

"My name is What-the-blazing-hell-do-you-think-you're-doin'-showing-up-in-our-town-brawlin'?" I narrowed my eyes dangerously at both of them, untrusting also of the mischief twinkling through the raven-haired man's blue eyes.

"What's *your* name?" I asked the blond, swallowing my satisfied smile while I waited. I'm pretty sure we all did.

By now, a crowd of cowboys, cowgirls, assorted magical creatures, and some horses had formed a circle around us.

The blond gave what I'm sure he thought was a slow spread of seduction via a smile that curved his full lips. It only made me more cautious of him. By default, I was wary of everything that came in too pretty a package.

"Well, beautiful," he said as he took a couple of steps toward me. When Tiger growled at him, he halted, proving he wasn't all stupid. "My name's Rhett Steed."

I and everyone else within view around us smiled at the consternation tugging on his brow.

He shook his head. "No, that's not my name. That's not it at all. I'm Rhett Steed." He pursed his lips while his brow drew so low that it shaded his troubled eyes. "Rhett Steed. Rhett Steed."

When he glanced up and caught our grins, he plopped both hands on his narrow waist with an angry jerk. "My name's Rhett Steed."

Most newcomers embraced shock for longer than this, but he just got madder than Tiger when I took away his food. Rhett glared at the other man as if he were the source of his new name.

"What'd you do now, you motherflipper?"

Those brows dipped until they almost tangled with his long lashes. "You motherflapper. You fretting fat flasher!"

Then he glowered at me so hard I worried he might break something inside—until I remembered he deserved it for all his ogling.

I batted my own long eyelashes at him, fluttering pure innocence.

His nostrils flaring, he snapped his head toward the raven-haired god, whose own bright lips were pursed tightly together.

"What the fritter in hell's *your* name?" Rhett barked.

Forehead creasing in anticipation of what he figured was to come, proving he wasn't as idiotic as he'd seemed either, he said, "It's Zeke Doyle."

"No it's flapping not," Rhett growled. "And why can't I farting cuss?"

Tilting my head to the side while I scratched behind Tiger's ears, I smiled sweetly. "Welcome to Traitor's Den, gentlemen, where you're made to mind your manners. Most of the time, anyhow."

Without further explanation, though Rhett and Zeke would need much of it to understand the peculiar rules that controlled our small town, I sauntered off, feeling both their stares following me until I reached Jolene, and the circle of townies closed around them, all but swallowing them up with a barrage of questions and little of the manners I'd just touted.

CHAPTER 3

*You Need Something Stronger Than a Good Roll in the Hay*

I had ample time to show Jolene some appreciation, giving her a hose-down and hay, along with water for Tiger, who hunted for his own food, before the first trickle of townies began returning from the border abuzz with talk of the portal and the two newest members of Traitor's Den.

Tiger snoozed at my feet, his enormous head resting on his equally sizable paws, while I kicked back once more at my favorite table in Sharmayne's Den. I always chose the same seat for its view of the entire establishment and the large windows that bordered the street.

It was through these windows that I spotted Rhett and Zeke arriving outside. Rhett rode behind

Hank Henry, looking like he'd never been in a saddle before, and mighty displeased about the arrangement. Zeke rode behind Letitia Lake, which didn't surprise me in the least. She was leaning back in the saddle so she was pressed against Zeke's chest, forcing him to circle his arms around her waist to keep from falling off her horse. That woman had wedged herself between nearly as many couples as the mayor had, only she didn't bother hiding her true intentions. She was all fluffed hair, gigantic earrings, and skin-tight jeans. She also pushed the boundaries of her brassiere on a daily basis, defying the ratio of how much boob must remain behind fabric without the rest spilling out all over whatever schmo she was putting the moves on.

All atop their own horses, a parade of Denners circled the new arrivals.

A moderate to mediocre wizard, Hank appeared tickled pink to be the center of attention, even if more eyes were on Zeke and even Chester Bo than him. Chester Bo was a Morgan with a shiny black coat and matching tail and mane, far better suited to the Wild West—or Traitor's Den's version of it, anyhow—than Hank Henry would ever be, no matter how many times he waltzed through town in his chaps and button-down shirts with fringe all along the chest.

Rhett's handsome face pinched in irritation as he swung a leg, trying to dismount without touching Hank Henry. He kneed Hank in the back, then kicked Chester Bo in the flank, making the horse whinny and jump, before finally sliding down the Morgan's side.

"At least it's not my job to teach them how to ride," I commented to Tiger while I chuckled at the show Rhett was unintentionally putting on. Tiger's cheek twitched in his sleep, his long whiskers bobbing.

As much trouble as Rhett had dismounting, Zeke was having more. And it wasn't because of Cinnamon Cream, Letitia's unassuming cinnamon-colored mare.

Zeke was trying to get down while Letitia was busy pretending she didn't notice, leaning so far back against him her head was nearly in his lap.

Sharmayne, who'd been in the process of sliding a Moon Mixer across the table at me, noticed and tsked loudly enough to draw the attention of the few patrons willing to abandon the entertainment outside to secure the best tables.

"That woman's nose is pointed so high up she'd

well and drown in a rainstorm. A light one too, mind you. She thinks her shit don't stink and everybody wants her."

I didn't think Letitia threw herself at any man with two legs and dangly bits between them because she had a case of overconfidence, but I'd long ago learned not to debate such things with the bar matron.

Zeke finally managed to swing his left leg around the back of the horse, but when he tried to slide down and off, Letitia swiveled quickly, leaning up and out of her saddle, trying to hold on to him with the pretense of offering him a hand.

That gave Sharmayne—and the rest of the saloon's patrons—a clear shot of round Letitia behind.

Again, Sharmayne tsked while also shaking her head. "Those pants a hers she wears are so tight I can see clear from here to next Tuesday and back again. No wonder she can't keep a good man. No man wants the cow when he can get the milk for free. That's plain common sense."

When Sharmayne whirled to look at me, I hmmmmed noncommittally. Letitia was far from my favorite person in town, but to each their own. She wanted to be a hussy? Well, a hussy she was, and she was damn good at it too.

When Sharmayne looked unsatisfied at my contribution to her condemnation, loud enough for every other patron to hear, I drank a long, cold sip of Moon Mixer, humming in genuine appreciation this time.

I licked my upper lip. "Mmmm, mmmm, Shar. I don't know how you do it, but I tell ya, no one makes a drink like you do."

A blush swept across Sharmayne's cheeks as if she didn't all but have a monopoly on the booze in town. She lifted loose tendrils of hair from her neck as if the heat were the cause of her suddenly rosy cheeks.

"Mmm, mmmmm. So damn good." I downed a third of my drink and smiled.

She tapped my table. "Let me get you a taste of something new I've been workin' on. You tell me what you think."

My smile tightened, but I didn't drop it. I was busy hoping the new concoction was awesome, because if not I was going to have to pretend it was.

She'd just returned with a shot glass filled with fuchsia pink swirling liquid and placed it in front of me when the doors swung open and Rhett rushed in, scanning the place before spotting me and heading my way.

Zeke entered moments behind him, Letitia all but lunging off Cinnamon Cream headfirst to follow.

Rhett pulled out one of the empty chairs and sat without saying a word.

I raised a single, accusing eyebrow. The one-brow move had taken me years of practice, but I had it down now.

On the floor beside me, Tiger's breathing grew shallower. My fiercest protector was now awake and giving his full attention even if he didn't look it.

Zeke arrived at my side a moment later, startled at the full-grown tiger partially tucked beneath the table, and looked at me, his throat visibly bobbing. "Um, is this seat taken?"

Instead of answering, I looked at Rhett. "See? That's what one's supposed to say before taking a seat at a lady's table."

Rhett's smile didn't reach his eyes. "Forgive me if I'm a bit overwhelmed by my sudden"—he quickly scanned the saloon—"new surroundings."

Sharmayne's saloon was dusty despite her continual efforts to exorcise her worst enemy, but we lived smack dab in the middle of a desert. There was dirt, dirt, and more dirt, as far as the eye could see in all directions, save the river, the one sparing grace of the town.

Beyond the ubiquitous dust, Sharmayne kept her bar tidy, her patrons well trained. They pulled out a chair, she expected them to push it back in when they left. They spilled, she expected them to call her so she could wipe it up before it left a sticky residue on her tables. The lavs were out of toilet paper? Then she damn well expected the patron to put on one of the new rolls she kept in a handy stack before they left the loo.

While Rhett continued to study the saloon, his eyes slid to the stairs at the back of the room behind us that led to the second floor.

I turned to Zeke. "You may sit. Thank you for having the good manners to ask first, like you bloody well should."

Zeke's hand already on the back of the chair, he paused. "And the, um, tiger? He won't...?" He trailed off.

"Eat you? Naw. Tiger's as gentle as a pussycat." This, of course, was a flat-out lie. Every Denner knew it. Tiger would surely know it was a joke and not bother taking offense.

"Quite a large fellow for a pussycat, isn't he?" Zeke asked as he pulled out the chair and sat.

"You should hear his meow." It rattled windows and doors on their hinges. Sometimes, when Tiger was particularly frustrated, it would rattle Hettie Lou Lyn's teeth that sat loose in her gums.

Rhett drummed his fingers on the table. "So, we hear you're the person to see."

"Seems to me you've already done plenty lookin'."

Rhett smirked. "There's plenty to admire."

"Yeah, well, I'm sheriff around these here parts, so you might want to keep that in mind."

"Or what?"

That was a mighty fine question. I couldn't very well land him in the clink because he kept checking me out.

That's when Letitia reached us, flustered in her haste to claim the final empty chair at my table. Unlike Rhett, she knew better and hesitated, leaning on the back of the vacant chair.

"Hey, Loretta. This seat empty?"

"It looks pretty empty to me," Rhett grumbled, dismissing her, eyes back on me.

But Letitia really did know better. She waited.

"Sorry, Letitia. Nothin' personal, but we've gotta have us a little meetin', lay out some ground rules."

"And I can't be part of that?" It was a hopeful whine. Have some pride, woman, I felt like telling her.

"Not today, sorry." I offered her my unbending, I'm-done-with-you smile, and the unrelenting woman got the hint. I wasn't known for changing my mind once I made it.

"Alright, then. Catch ya later, boys," she said before sashaying away with so much swing to her hips that I briefly wondered if it was possible to dislodge one that way.

"We kept asking everyone what the hell's going on," Rhett said, "but they kept telling us to talk to you."

"While they had no problem asking us all their questions about who we are, which we didn't answer." Zeke rubbed at his neck, flicking a quick glance toward the windows. When he noticed Letitia staring at him with a fair amount of purpose in her gaze, he whipped his eyes back to me, both of them wide, revealing a stark, crystalline blue.

Sharmayne sidled back up to the table then, draping her rag over the open chair with a well-practiced flick. "What'll it be for you, boys?"

"What's with calling us 'boys?'" Rhett grumbled. He did a lot of that. "Seems to me we look pretty plainly like men—even him." His lip curled in evident distaste as he gestured toward Zeke.

"I'll call ya boys till you prove to me you're men. Till then, I reserve judgment."

Which was new for Sharmayne, who didn't reserve it for much of any reason.

"What'd you think?" she asked me, pointing with her head at the still untouched—and now bubbling—small glass of bright, hot pink liquor.

"Got distracted." But I took a tentative sip, letting the liquid slide across my tongue for a moment, then tossed the rest of it back in one gulp. "Holy spicy taco shimoly. Shar, that's freaking fantastic." I smacked my lips, ignoring the way I felt both Rhett and Zeke's attention on my mouth. "It's like ... cotton candy ... and caramel ... and I dunno, but it tastes as good as a fine roll in the hay."

Sharmayne's grin was all blinding teeth, except for the one crooked one in the front. "I think that's what I'll call it. Roll in the Hay."

"Can I have one of those, then?" Rhett asked. "I could use some"—his eyes skimmed the length of me above the table—"release and relaxation. A good roll in the hay…"

"Don't you go eyeing our Loretta like that. She's got a beau, and a mighty fine man our Cole is too."

"Are they married?" Rhett asked.

"Not yet. But soon."

I pursed my lips at Sharmayne, but she didn't pay me any mind. Cole had been asking me to marry him at least twice a season since we were fifteen. I hadn't said yes yet. Wasn't sure I ever would, though Sharmayne was right. He was a very good man.

Gaze hot and pinned on me, Rhett went on. "Okay ... so if I can't have Loretta"—his eyes flared, suggesting he didn't believe for a second he couldn't get me one way or another—"can I at least have one of them pretty drinks? A Roll in the Hay?" He let the words dance across his tongue.

I rolled my eyes. "You're gonna need something a hell of a lot stronger than a Roll in the Hay when I tell you what you've both just gotten yourselves into. Trust me on that."

"Right." Sharmayne nodded, suddenly all business. "Two Sirens on the Rocks coming up."

Then, with a flare of compassion, she patted her open palm along the table. "You might want to wait to take a few sips before Loretta tells you anything. I'll hurry it up."

That got Rhett and Zeke's attention, all right.

Not only they, but every nearby patron in the saloon, which was now busting at the seams, leaned forward, waiting for me to begin to tell the story every Denner had heard many times over.

The story never changed.

Because none of us ever got out.

## CHAPTER 4
## Uncle Tucker's Western Theme Park Calls for Moonshine

Rhett and Zeke sat with their Sirens on the Rocks half empty, dripping condensation onto the table in front of them. I downed the rest of my Moon Mixer, signaled Sharmayne for another, and began.

"You've arrived in a town called Traitor's Den, and I hope you like it, 'cause you won't be leaving anytime soon. And by that, I really mean never. Like, you might want to get nice and cozy here. Unless … do you happen to know my Uncle Tucker?"

"Who the hell is this Tucker everyone keeps asking about?" growled Rhett once more, making me think he must be a shifter of some sort. Shifters as a whole tended to be growly types, didn't matter what color their stripes or spots were.

Before I could answer Rhett, Zeke, forehead furrowed, asked, "Traitor's Den? We passed a welcome sign on our way here, and it announced the town as 'Raitor's Den.'"

I waved a hand in the air between us. "Oh. That. Yeah. Many of us around these here parts don't take too kindly to being referred to as traitors when we aren't. Even those who are traitors seem not to like it—which reminds me, you'll also have to meet our mayor. He likes being part of our welcoming committee."

"No one mentioned the mayor." Rhett scanned our many spectators, but there wasn't a single apologetic look among them, though there were a few unconcerned shrugs.

"Anyhoo," I started back up, my obligatory mention of our fine mayor now complete. "This is a magical town, you might've noticed."

"No, we hadn't," Rhett said, causing a few in our audience to scowl openly at him.

I'd warn him to be careful of what he said, that even though this town was forced on us and not a single one of us lived here by choice, we still took a certain amount of pride in our home. Like prize-winning champs, we made the best of a crappy situation—most of us did, anyhow.

But Rhett was a grown man. All that sexy scruff on his chin and those developed muscles assured it. If he wasn't interested in making friends, that was on him. I was a sheriff, not a babysitter, not even for the newbies.

"It is indeed a magical town. A very magical town. And our welcome sign is governed by the spell set up by my Uncle Tucker. It's supposed to say, 'Traitor's Den,' but since we don't take too kindly to that, we take turns defacing the T." I took a sip of my Moon Mixer. "It doesn't take all that long for the T to reappear, but until then we get to be 'raitors' instead of 'traitors.' Make sense?"

"No," Rhett said.

"None," Zeke echoed.

"Dandy," I said with some pep, causing Rhett to growl at me again. If he didn't watch himself, he was going to get Tiger growling back at him, and Tiger's growl was actually something to be concerned about.

Tiger's left shoulder was already twitching. Though his eyes still remained closed, it was a sure sign he was annoyed.

Noticing Levi and Collette Ray enter, also known as Daddy and Momma, I waved at them. They waved back and slipped into the crowd, always mindful not to interfere when I was acting in an official capacity.

"The pocket portal you entered, the entire town you see here, everything inside it—save us—is an invention of my Uncle Tucker, my dad's brother. I never met him, but he's a wizard with powerful creation magic. Clearly. He made this whole place to trap my dad in it. That's why everyone keeps asking if you know my Uncle Tucker. Best we can figure, he's the only one who can let us all out of here."

I paused, taking in the shock freezing Zeke's face, and the way the same emotion made Rhett's cheeks heat with frustration—or maybe that was plain ol' anger.

"You're kidding, right?" Zeke asked with a fair amount of hope.

"Nope. Not even a smidgen. Though I do enjoy a good joke as much as the rest, maybe more. Now, just to be certain, you do *not* know Tucker Ray?"

"Never even heard of him," Rhett said.

"Me neither," Zeke said. "Though I'm not sure I would've. I don't travel in the same circles as mages."

"Nor do I," Rhett said. "In my experience, they're mostly a bunch of jerkwads."

Chairs squeaked as they scraped across the floor. A dozen or so men and women—*mages*—stood.

"Hm," I murmured. "You might want to wait till I finish telling you the whole story before you go making enemies. As you can see, we have lots of witches and wizards in our town. Most of them are fine folk."

"And the rest of them?" Zeke asked.

I shrugged and took another sip of my Moon Mixer, enjoying the sweet flavor despite all the sour vibes Rhett was putting off. "I'll put it this way. We all ended up here by accident. But by and large, we've all got a bit of a rebel streak in us. Seems the magic governing our fine town here brings it out in us. There's a fair amount of trouble and mischief, which is why I'm the sheriff."

"And why you in particular?" Zeke asked.

"Because she's damn good at the job," someone hollered from the crowd. I thought it might be Bobbie Sue, but I couldn't be sure.

Just in case, I smiled my thanks at Bobbie Sue, whom I couldn't see. "I take my job seriously. So long as we're stuck here, I make sure things are fair for everyone. Or fair enough, anyhow. Can't be too strict."

"And why not?" Rhett asked.

"Because, in case you didn't notice, my Uncle

Tucker based this entire town on a Wild West theme."

"Meaning?" Zeke pressed.

"Meaning Tucker created the pocket portal out of nothing, right? Using his magic. Only people with magic of their own, and enough of it, best we can figure, can see the pocket portal to begin with. Same for entering it. You don't got magic, ya ain't getting in. Course, y'all don't know that once you walk through it there's no getting back out. There ain't a warning sign or a disclaimer or nothin'. You're good and stuck once you get through the pocket portal."

"Has anyone tried to get back out?" Zeke asked.

I frowned. "What do you think? Course we've tried. Lots of times. Lots and lots and lots of times. But you saw, the portal disappears and that's that. We've done everything we can think of to try to summon it back, including magic of our own. If you can think of it, we've tried it. Guaranteed. And you saw—or wait, maybe you didn't see since you were busy being idjits, fightin' each other. But Ashton Blu actually made it through the portal this time."

"And the bottle," Bobbie Sue called out.

"Right. And the bottle. They both came flying back out, spit out by the portal like one of us 'bout swallowing a fly."

"Well, *I* haven't tried yet," said Rhett.

"I see. And you think your shit smells like roses?"

"Maybe it does."

"Well, you feel free to try all you want. We have a rotating schedule of us who keep watch, just in case the portal opens back up, so we can try sending someone and a message through again."

"Even though this Ashton and the bottle didn't quite work this time?" Zeke asked.

"We Denners are good at one thing, and that's not giving up."

"Hear, hear!" someone called out to a chorus of cheers.

Eyeing their still half-full drinks, I shook my head a bit, mildly impressed despite myself. "You two are taking the news well."

"That's because we aren't buying it," Rhett said.

Just like that, I was no longer impressed. "Well, then it's a damn good thing I ain't trying to sell a thing. And if that's the way you're gonna be about it—"

"Please don't rope me in with him," Zeke interjected. "That's what got me into this mess in the first place. Rhett Steed does *not* speak for me, never has, even when he went by another name."

"You got it," I told him. "In this town here, we

all take responsibility for our own actions. I make sure of it. That's my job."

"Go, Loretta!" another voice hollered, and this time I wasn't sure who it was. The townies weren't usually this openly supportive of me. But one thing this town did well was come together when necessary, and right now it seemed the Denners were perceiving the new arrivals, probably mostly Rhett, as a threat to me.

Rhett snorted. "Got a little cheering section, don't you? Do you make them say that stuff? Part of your little welcome speech?"

At that, the crowd went eerily still and silent. All but Tiger and Jolene. Jolene whinnied her protest outside, but Tiger was my immediate concern. As he rose to his large, heavy paws, I placed a calming hand on his head and kept it there.

"It's okay, Tiger. I got this."

A low rumble rolled deep in his chest.

Rhett had the good sense to appear intimidated, though he hid it well. The tension in his jaw and the mild tic in one eye gave him away.

Zeke didn't bother to hide his apprehension, sliding his chair back from the table to more clearly distance himself from the jackass with a stupid retort on the tip of his tongue for just about everything.

Keeping one hand on Tiger, I slid my drink to the side with the other, and leaned on the table, closing the distance between Rhett and me.

Up close, it was easier to make out that his eyes weren't a flat forest green; flecks of yellow, blue, and brown made them so much more interesting. His face was beautiful and yet still masculine, his square jaw reinforcing the manly aspect of his features.

Too bad he was one of the biggest jerkwads to ever come through the portal.

Dropping my voice so it vibrated with all the danger I was purposefully injecting into it, with a cold smile, I said, "Here in Traitor's Den, we're all judged on our actions. Not where we came from, not what we did before, not who we used to know. Connections from the outside world won't help you here. In here, you earn your reputation, fair and square. If I have a cheering squad, it's because I put the needs of others first as much as I should. I give respect when it's earned and treat everyone fairly. You treat others like shit, you'll have me to deal with, and trust me, so far you've only seen my nice side. Mess with me or my Denners and I'll come after you and make sure you never make that same mistake again."

Rhett snorted as if what I said were a joke.

"I guess you're either more thickheaded than you look, or your mind don't work as good as it should. You'd better mind your step, mister, or you're gonna end up regrettin' it. Big time."

Casually, as if I hadn't just more or less threatened him, Rhett took an easy sip of his Sirens on the Rocks. Ice clinked at the bottom of his mug while ocean blue liquid poured into his mouth. He swallowed a grimace I knew he must feel. Sharmayne went heavy on the moonshine for this bomb of a drink; it had to be burning down his throat all the way to his belly. His flat, muscled belly, I'd bet—the asshole.

"You get what I'm telling you here?" I pressed.

"I hear you, all right. Hard to miss all the bluster."

Tiger growled so loudly the windows at the front of the saloon shook, and the drinking glasses on tables trembled. Outside, horses neighed in camaraderie.

"It's okay, Tiger," I told my trusted companion. "I'm about to show this dumbass why he shouldn't mess with me."

Pushing my chair back, I stood. "We're taking this outside. One rule that's fixed in town, we don't mess up Sharmayne's saloon. Ever."

"That's right, Loretta," Sharmayne said. "You go show him who's boss now."

Zeke stood too, holding out a calming hand. "Just a minute. Before you go beat his ass, which I agree he fully deserves, will you finish telling me the rest of what I need to know? Please? I still don't understand ... exactly."

I eyed Zeke. His dark hair made his light skin appear lighter and his blue eyes brighter. That pale skin wouldn't last long under the relentless beating sun of the desert.

Wagging my lips back and forth, I considered him. "You know what? You got it. Rhett will still be here after I finish informing you, and that's a definite. Besides, now I'm kind of wishing I hadn't stepped between the two of you. I get exactly why you came through the pocket portal pummeling his ass."

Zeke sat. "Thank you kindly."

I sat too. Tiger, however, did not, stalking forward until his nose was a hot breath away from Rhett's shoulder.

Rhett eyed Tiger warily, suggesting for the first time that maybe he did have at least a smidgen of common sense after all.

"What's his deal?" Zeke asked for Rhett, who must have had the question on the tip of his tongue.

"Tiger's a shifter, but he got stuck in his creature form for some reason. We don't know how or why, and since he can't talk..."

"How do you know he's a shifter and not just a regular ol' tiger?" Zeke shifted closer to the table so he could better study the magical creature over it.

"It's like they ain't even listenin'." Sharmayne's comment reached us, causing Zeke to tense in reaction. But Rhett didn't stop staring back at Tiger, whose lethal glare was probably beginning to burn a hole in the man's psyche.

"Tiger has to be a shifter stuck in his creature form because you can only get through the portal if you have magic," I said. *Duh.* Hadn't I told them that already?

"Could he not be a regular person—not a shifter —with a spell placed on him?" Zeke asked, and a flutter of interest circled the room. Those Denners who hadn't been able to fit inside pressed their faces to the front windows as they listened through the open doorway to the saloon.

"Hmm," I finally said, with a questioning look at Tiger. "Never thought of that one."

Rhett snorted. I silently wondered whether

maybe I should kill him and spare the rest of the town from his attitude problem.

Ignoring Rhett, only for now, I continued to address Zeke. "I suppose it's possible a spell could register as enough magic for the pocket portal. Though none of us know all the dos and don'ts of the thing. Whaddya say, Tiger? Are you a regular ol' human with a spell on you?"

Tiger turned his head my way, chuffed, and shook it in the negative.

"So still a shifter stuck in his creature form?"

Tiger nodded several times before turning back to his intimidating glaring at the jerkwad the town's spell had decided to name Rhett. Had I been consulted, I would've chosen something far more colorful and personality appropriate. Like Dick.

Giving Rhett much of my back, I told Zeke, "When someone enters this town, the magic gives them a new name. Most of them are Western themed, but sometimes they're just weird. Everything in the Den is a bit odd, you'll soon find."

Zeke glanced around us. "That's already starting to become clear."

There were witches and wizards, yes, but also shifters of all types—plus a dwarf, a few fairies, a gnome, and a pygmy troll had joined us a couple of years ago. I could just make out the tip of his bright violet fro-hawk among the crowd. And the koala who'd ambled her way through the portal currently perched on Cole's shoulder as he pushed through the throng. The magical creature was shy and preferred to hitch rides with Denners instead of standing on her own.

"So y'all get new names, and the spell keeps you from even saying the one you had before. We can't drop the F-bomb, no matter how creatively we try to enmesh it into phrases—trust me on this, we've tried—and the longer you live here, the more of a Westerner you become."

I chuckled ruefully. "Not sure my Uncle Tucker knew all that much about what a Wild West town is supposed to look like, so we got a theatrical, modified, kinda theme-park version of it. Whatever he imagined, I guess. We have electricity and running water, via his lasting magic, and other things like that. After a quick settling-in period, you'll be expected to contribute. Jim Bob Two—"

Rhett snorted. I ignored him, though I did mentally tack on an extra bullet to the shin for later.

I cleared my throat. "Jim Bob Two is our town accountant. The saloon, the general store, the hardware store, the eateries, all of 'em, they keep a tab for us. Jim Bob Two tallies what our contributions are worth, and every once in a while he adds everything up for each of us, keeping us all on course."

"He's fair as fair gets," a Denner piped up.

"Yep. He is," I said. "You'll each get a roof over your head and a horse and a hat to start, and we'll go from there. I'm all tuckered out from talking. We can figure out the rest later. I've got an ass to kick."

I stood again.

"And how many people are stuck in this place?" Rhett asked.

Huffing, I looked down at him. "With the addition of the two of you, and minusing the two who died, we're at an even ... three-hundred-and-sixty-nine. Am I right, folks?"

"Yep, that's right, honey," my dad said, weaving between the crowd to draw closer.

"This is my dad," I told the new men. "Levi Ray."

Even after sizing up my dad, Rhett still said, "And he's the one to blame for all this?"

Levi Ray was a black bear shifter. Now, black bears are smaller than grizzlies, but they're still *bears*. Proving, once more, that of our newest residents, half of them was a damn fool.

Everyone, even Lonnie Marr, who, bless him, was

a little slow on the take, knew better than to enrage a bear of any sort.

"Yes I am," my dad said, never one to shirk responsibility. He'd decided long ago he was entirely to blame for everyone's misfortune of ending up stuck here forever. "Now, we should move this outside. My daughter's been trying to give you the lowdown out of the kindness of her big heart. But you'll have to make do without the rest. I, for one, don't like how you're talkin' to her, and I've lost patience with waiting for her to kick your ass. And yes, she can take care of herself, but when you mess with someone I love, you mess with me too. She's first. I'm next."

"And I'm after you," Cole said, already handing off the timid koala to Sharmayne.

"Can I still get a shot at him?" Zeke asked. "I have unfinished business with him too."

"Can't wait to hear about it," my dad said, before pointing at Rhett. "You. Out. Now."

Tiger pushed Rhett's shoulder with his nose, causing it to slide from the armrest to his lap.

Rhett huffed, as if everyone else were the jerk instead of him. "Fine." He threw his hands in the air. "Flipping face fanny, *fine*." He grimaced at the unpleasant substitutions for what were surely attempts at far more pleasant F-bombs. "You want to have at me? Go for it. But you haven't asked me what *I* turn into."

With that ominous statement, he rose and stalked through the quickly parting crowd and out into the blazing sunshine that was as constant in Traitor's Den as its magic.

I downed what was left of my Moon Mixer and rose to follow.

No Denner ever backed down from a fight, not even not-all-there Lonnie Marr or old-as-dirt Hettie Lou Lyn.

The law of Traitor's Den was the same as the Wild West. Just our version of it.

Rhett hadn't asked *me* about *that* either.

## CHAPTER 5
### *Size Doesn't Matter, or You Get Dynamited*

Whoever hadn't been able to squeeze into Sharmayne's saloon, which was most Denners, caught on quickly enough as to what was happening, and hustled into the street, aiming to get a front-row view of the upcoming showdown. Since the dirt thoroughfare was wide, they remained light on their feet, ready to move depending on where I ended up standing.

But I wasn't the town's favorite sheriff—okay, *only* sheriff the town had ever had—because I didn't notice these kinds of things.

After I settled in the middle of the street, facing away from the sun so I didn't have to squint, and Tiger, Daddy, Momma, Cole, and, surprisingly, Zeke, lined up behind me, along with a whole bunch of Denners, I announced, "If you got a good seat to Rhett being a butt before, be kind to your neighbor and let them shimmy up ahead of you now."

I didn't, however, enforce my suggestion. I made sure to be a fair sheriff, but that didn't mean I was a hand holder. I had far better things to do than that, even if it was just to sit back in my favorite chair in Sharmayne's place and kick up my feet.

Rhett squared off in front of me, finally appearing appropriately wary, casting narrow-eyed glances at everyone, especially me. Or maybe that was just the sun in his eyes.

Only those Denners who hadn't been able to snag a good vantage point on my side of things lined the street beside Rhett.

"This is a bit savage, wouldn't you say?" Rhett asked of me. "We just arrived. Seems like there should be an allowance for shock and the like. A grace period."

I cocked a hip, petting my six shooter, the one loaded with silver bullets. *Big Wilma*. If he was a shifter, then silver bullets were the only ones that'd do much more than tickle his balls.

"You strike me as the savage type, Mister Steed."

His responding grin assured that I'd pegged him right. "I prefer to be on the side of dealing the savagery, not receiving it." He raised a brow. "Is this a duel to the death? If so, it doesn't seem like a fair fight since you have those cannons strapped to your hips."

"If you're asking if I'm gonna slice your head off or carve out your heart and feed it to Tiger..." I offered him my own vicious grin. "Then no, not this time. And that's the only way you can die, ain't that so?"

Slowly, he nodded.

"Well, then, you got nothin' to worry about. Besides, I'm sure someone'll lend you one of their guns till you can get one of your own."

En masse, those Denners surrounding him took a long step back. Every one of them would be packing at least one revolver. Even Sharmayne, who'd been last to bustle out of her saloon, was shaking her head. Though she wore flowered dresses and dainty aprons bordered in lace, she carried a ladylike firearm in one of her apron's pockets. And since she only carried one weapon on her person—otherwise relying on a shotgun behind the bar—it'd be loaded with silver bullets.

No Denner, not even Lonnie or Hettie Lou Lyn, would be caught dead unarmed.

Rhett took in the even wider gap now separating

him from the rest of the Denners. "I see the people here are the generous sort."

"Here in Traitor's Den," Hank Henry called out loudly, chest puffed out with importance, "you get the treatment ya earn. You should turn that accusing look on yourself, Mister Steed."

"Will everyone *stop* calling me that? That's not my name."

I shrugged. "It is now."

"It will be till ya die," Bobbie Sue said, fluffing her red curls matter-of-factly.

"Just 'cause *you* haven't figured a way out of here doesn't mean I won't."

"Not gonna lie, I like your confidence," I said. "I hope you do find a way out. We all do."

"Sure do," Saxon Silver said as he petted his long, thick beard. "We'll even forgive you for bein' a turd if you find us all a way out of this blasted place. I miss my mines."

"A ... dwarf?" Rhett asked in the kind of condescending way that no one ever addressed Saxon Silver. You know, because we had two working eyes —at least most of us did—and some functioning common sense.

Saxon looked like he was about to wrestle me for the privilege of teaching Rhett a lesson.

The dwarf, all nearly-four-feet of him, stomped several menacing steps toward Rhett. "What'd you just say to me?"

"I called you a dwarf. But you can't possibly be insulted by that since it's what you are, isn't it?"

"Oh, so now you're telling me what I can and can't take offense from?"

Anyone within an arm's length of Saxon took several steps backward.

Saxon moved toward Rhett, reducing the distance between the explosive blacksmith slash jeweler and the new town idjit.

"Of course I'm a dwarf, what else would I be? It's how you said that I'm a dwarf, like there's something wrong with that. What's wrong with being a dwarf, huh? What's wrong with it?"

Rhett shrugged, like he didn't have a care in the world. "You're really short."

While Saxon fumed and his face grew red behind all the bushy facial hair, I glanced over my shoulder at Zeke. "Is he stupid or something? Like for real stupid, not just me saying it. Like maybe it's a medical condition?"

For once, I wasn't jesting. It was a sudden concern. Was I about to let a mentally challenged man get beat up because he couldn't understand when not to poke the enraged bears, both literally and figuratively?

Zeke stood, arms crossed over his chest, squinty eyes pinned on his rival, and it wasn't from the sun. "Nope. He's the most arrogant man I've ever met. He never thinks before he speaks, and he acts before questioning his choices. But he's all there in the head." He pushed his lips out while he considered the man in question. "At least ... I think he is. I've witnessed him behave in remarkably intelligent fashion before."

"So maybe that was the exception to the rule?" my mom asked. "Seems to me like the porch light's on but no one's home. No one in their right mind would purposefully antagonize Saxon Silver."

"He's a *dwarf*," Cole emphasized.

But if Zeke didn't realize that dwarves were stubborn as stubborn got and that they never, ever let go of a grudge, then he wouldn't understand.

"And he's the only one in town who makes bullets of any kind," my dad added.

At that, Zeke nodded in understanding, then shrugged. "Well, then seems to me that Rhett's about to learn a lesson that I was hoping to teach him. But I don't mind waiting. I'll enjoy watching."

From the look of the rest of the Denners, I suspected we all would.

Saxon finally moved past his fury to sputter, "Me 'n you are gonna mix. Boy, are we ever gonna mix." He brought up his hands in tight fists and started moving in, bouncing on kid-sized cowboy boots that were tucked into his jeans.

Rhett brought up his palms. "I'm not going to fight you. It wouldn't be a fair fight."

Saxon froze, fists still in the air.

I barely breathed, anticipating the explosion I knew was coming.

Every Denner there waited to see what Saxon would do. We'd never seen anyone push his buttons like this. We all knew better.

"*You* ... fighting *me* ... wouldn't be a fair fight?" It wasn't so much a question as a statement loaded with enough dynamite to blow a hole clear through town.

"Obviously not. I'm a man of ... some honor."

Zeke snorted while Saxon repeated, in that same tone fraught with more danger than a "WARNING: DYNAMITE" sign: "Obviously not."

"Well, yeah. Look at you and look at me."

"Can't help but," Saxon said. "I'm tryin' to figure out if your butthole somehow got switched with your mouth when you came through the portal. Somethin' to make sense of what you're sayin' to me."

Quickly dismissing the imagery I had no desire to focus on, I walked closer to the two men in the middle of the street, visibly throwing my support behind Saxon—but not so close that he'd think I believed him incapable of handing the idjit his ass on a platter.

Saxon was fully capable. He was fierce and highly dedicated to his craft. He was the sole reason I was considering shooting Rhett in both shins just to shut him up already.

Rhett held his hands up in front of him once more, as if he were inoffensive. But he kept opening his mouth and sticking both feet right in, starting with the tips of his brand new, shiny black cowboy boots, courtesy of Uncle Tucker's magic.

"I just mean," Rhett said, "I'm bigger and stronger than you is all. I'd hurt you if we fight, and I don't want to do that. I like to look out for the little guy."

A collective gasp circled the onlookers, and I stepped back again.

"Well, this is about to get ugly," I breathed, and

Cole stepped between my parents to slide his arm around my waist.

He leaned his lips next to my ear. "Looks like you won't have to put this idjit in his place after all. Saxon's liable not to even leave scraps."

Saxon was, indeed, snarling as viciously as any animal, bouncing around on his feet in an agitated frenzy.

Rhett scoffed at him then brought his hands to his hips. "Fine. If you won't listen to reason"—another collective gasp swept across us Denners while Tiger pressed against my free side—"then we should at least use guns. So size doesn't matter."

Size didn't matter. We all knew that. Well, all but the *idjit*, which I was starting to think would stick as his new nickname. It was all about how you used what you were given, not just the size.

Rhett was saying size *did* matter.

And he was going to pay for that.

I blinked and Saxon was halfway at him. I blinked again, and Saxon was launching himself at the idjit from several feet away. His momentum made Rhett stumble while trying to grab at the dwarf. Saxon held on to the idjit's knees and tugged.

Like a tree, Rhett was about to topple, and Saxon

helped him along the way, ramming his head into Rhett's legs like a charging bull.

Rhett fell.

He'd barely landed when Saxon jumped on top of him, straddling his shoulders and pummeling his face with those agile hands of his.

No one said much as the sounds of flesh smashing into flesh colored the dense, late afternoon air.

"Maybe we should stop him," my mom said. "Saxon's hands are pretty valuable."

"They really are," Cole agreed. But no one moved.

It wasn't like Saxon was going to kill Rhett this way. Rhett was a shifter of some sort, which meant supernatural healing. He was literally impossible to kill like this.

When blood splattered Saxon's face, the crowd as a whole shifted from one leg to the other or twitched in some way.

When Rhett grabbed Saxon's waist with both hands, ripped him away, and threw him like he weighed no more than a sack of potatoes, we all moved.

Saxon bounced once, twice, three times, tucked, rolled, and reclaimed his feet. With one swift turn he was charging toward the idjit, who sat up, rubbing at his bloody face.

That's when I noticed that Kiki the Koala had climbed down Sharmayne's body and was ambling straight toward the shitfest. If Saxon had meant to teach Rhett a lesson before, after throwing him, Saxon would be looking to murder the idjit—or just short of it.

"Kiki," I whispered, and surprised glances followed my cautioning. Tiger chuffed his own warning.

"Watch out," Letitia yelled, for once prioritizing something other than trying to conquer one man or another. "Kiki's comin'!"

Saxon stopped running, eyes big beneath thick, bushy eyebrows. "Kiki?" he said softly, watching while she ambled right up to Rhett, peered up at him, seemed to ignore the smeared blood and murderous slant of his mouth, and climbed up his leg to hug his thigh.

"Well, butter my butt and call me a biscuit," my mom said from behind me.

"That about sums it up," I said. "Kiki's compass is all wonky."

Only, Kiki's inner compass was unlikely to be wonky. The koala didn't speak, but she was all gentle movements and joyful laziness. If any of us had a chance at figuring out inner peace, true happiness, or any of that hogwash, she was our girl for the job.

"Damn," Saxon grumbled. "I can't beat him to a pulp now."

Kiki sighed a cute koala sigh, closed her eyes, and held on.

"No, no you can't," I said.

"None of us can," my dad said, sounding mighty displeased about the fact.

"Damn him," Zeke said. "Why can't I just beat him up already?"

"That seems to be the existential question of the moment, now doesn't it?" I shook my head and forced my fingers away from Big Wilma.

No one in Traitor's Den was dying. Not today.

But I could still throw Rhett in the clink. The thought warmed my heart.

CHAPTER 6

*Bigger, Bulgier Problems Make for a Doozy*

Never had I received so many offers to become my sheriff's deputy. Of course, most of the offers were for just the one night, and the only ones of a more permanent nature came from Letitia Lake and Lonnie Marr—and a big *no* to them. I'd find Letitia in the cell with Rhett come morning, whether he liked it or not, and who knew what I might find Lonnie doing. He walked through life to the beat of his own drum.

I hadn't needed a deputy before and I sure as shit didn't need one now to babysit a snarly shifter of indeterminate nature—Rhett still wasn't spilling the beans.

But everyone wanted to witness me throwing Rhett in one of Traitor's Den's two jail cells. I'd only ever had to use one at a time, but the night was young, and already I was twitchy.

The front door to my office squeaked every time it opened and closed, and just about every Denner came through it at least once.

"Shouldn't I be on the receiving end of some good ol' fashioned Southern hospitality?" Rhett asked, face pressed between the bars of his prison in an attempt to look innocent or perhaps pitiful. He failed on both accounts. "Maybe a home-cooked meal, a cold beer, some good company?"

I snorted, leaning back in my chair, kicking my boots up on to my desk. My office was a single open space occupied by my desk, a couple of chairs on the other side of it, a few more against the opposite wall to serve as a waiting area, and the two cells. There was a lav back beside one of the cells and a filing cabinet where I kept records on all the troublemakers in town. It was full.

Cole, who hadn't left my side since the showdown in the street, rounded on Rhett with a menacing snarl curling his lip—and he wasn't even a shifter. "You want Southern hospitality? Then you'd better mosey on over to the South." Cole tilted his head as he studied the other man. "Have you really been so focused on your own winnin' personality not to notice anything around you?"

"If we're not in the South, then where the hell are we?"

I kicked my feet down to the floor with a loud slap, startling Tiger, who hadn't left my side either. Zeke was another one I hadn't been able to shake, but it was probably better he was here so I could keep an eye on both of the newcomers.

Standing, I approached Rhett's cell, Tiger mirroring my steps. "Have you not been listenin' at all? I *told* you where we are."

Of course, I had and I hadn't. We were smack dab in the middle of Traitor's Den, and there was no escaping it—all that was true. There was no chance of Rhett heading to the South or anywhere else. But not a single Denner knew exactly where we were. Not even our stellar mayor, who'd popped into my office only to make a brief appearance before heading off to the saloon. At least I didn't have to deal with him on my ass.

"I heard you all right," Rhett said. "But y'all act like—" He trailed off, eyes round. "I said 'y'all.'"

"Yep, ya sure did," Cole said with a smirk. Most new Denners handled the sudden onslaught of cowboy-isms—Uncle Tucker's theatrical version of them, anyway—with some good humor. Pretty sure Mister Steed here was incapable of it.

Voice filled with feigned innocence, I asked, "What were you about to say? We all act like ... what exactly?"

"Y'all"—his face puckered; even so, it didn't cease to be handsome, though I wished it had. He cleared his throat. "Y'all talk like you're from the South."

"No," Cole said. "We talk like we're from Traitor's Den. There's no place else like it."

This also was more of an assumption than an objective fact. Truth was, none of us knew more about Traitor's Den than we could guess. Though it seemed highly unlikely that there would be another place quite as uniquely odd as this one.

Zeke, who leaned against the bars of the neighboring cell, though from the outside, asked, "Where exactly are we, then?"

Tiger chuffed softly while I began walking aimlessly around the room. "If you're asking for map coordinates, we can't give 'em to you."

"We can't even be sure we popped out in the same dimension as the one we left," Cole added, causing both Rhett and Zeke to blink at us.

"*What?*" Rhett finally said, the single word standing out for its lack of inflection.

Cole shrugged, unconcerned, shoving strands of shaggy dark blond hair from his eyes. "Of course we don't know exactly where we are. The pocket portal spits us out here, and there ain't no homecomin' basket waitin' for us with a handy dandy instruction manual." Cole chuckled at his own joke. "The very nature of pocket portals is to be able to deliver the traveler just about anywhere. I'm luckier than a four-leaf clover that I ended up here."

With moony hazel eyes, Cole snagged my hand as I walked past, pulling me close. After gazing at me long enough to make me blush and wish we didn't have spectators, he added, "I was out looking for a pocket portal. They're not easy to find, you know. I finally stumbled on this one in the desert of Nevada, and here I am."

"We weren't in Nevada and we weren't looking for a portal, that's for damn sure," Zeke grumbled, whipping eye daggers at my prisoner. "If it weren't for him, I'd be home right now."

Rhett smiled like a feral animal, teeth bright and shiny. "Guess pampered pretty boy has to give up his palace. Who's gonna rub your feet now that you left all your slaves behind?"

Zeke's nostrils flared, though the rest of his face

remained dangerously still. "They aren't slaves. And it's not a palace."

"Whatever you say, *Prince*."

"I'm *not* a prince."

"Sure y'aren't. You can't get mad at me for calling a spade a spade."

"Perhaps not, since you do appear to wholly lack any common sense. But I can and *do* blame you for landing us here. If not for your lack of morals and *thievery*, we wouldn't be here."

Quietly, I nudged Tiger to follow and led Cole back to my desk area. If the newbies were gonna fight, then I'd let them. Prince? Palace? Slaves? I needed to know so much more, and the men had already revealed more in the few moments of squabbling than they had in answers to my earlier questions.

Rhett's fingers went white from how hard he gripped the bars on either side of his head. "It's not possible to steal something that should be yours in the first place. If anyone's a thief here, it's you."

Zeke sucked in an affronted breath. "Excuse you? Was *I* the one who broke into your home in the middle of the day and pilfered something that didn't belong to me? Was *I* the one who ran all over the damn country trying to disappear with stolen goods?"

Rhett's entire forehead rose an inch. "Goods? *Goods?* The egg isn't *goods*. But then, you'd know that if you were supposed to have it. You're not fit to be its guardian."

"Egg?" I whispered to Cole and Tiger, not wanting to interrupt them when they were in a good flow. But ... *egg*? That didn't sound particularly promising.

Zeke faced off with Rhett. If the bars hadn't been between them, I'd bet good money they'd be tumbling again.

"I'm fit to do far more than you ever will be," Zeke snarled, so intensely that his dark hair vibrated atop his head. "Everywhere you've ever gone, you've caused more trouble than you're worth. You've put yourself and no one else first for as long as you've been alive. *You* are the one who isn't fit to be a guardian. That egg won't remain an egg forever, and then what? You're going to be the one to raise it? Nurture and take care of it?"

"*It?*" I breathed. "Why do I have the feeling I'm not gonna like this?" I plopped into one of the chairs next to my desk, and Cole sat next to me, dragging his seat so close he was nearly on top of me. Tiger sank to the floor, his massive paws on top of my boots, his head atop them.

My guys were just being protective. I knew it. But I itched for some space I wouldn't be getting.

"It?" Rhett echoed. "See? You're not fit to raise him."

"It might not be a he. Just because you think with your dick more than your brain doesn't mean it's gonna be a male. Did you even stop to think about that?"

Rhett stiffened but didn't answer.

"I didn't think so. And what are you going to do if it's a she? You know what they say about the females."

Rhett huffed, but looked away, refusing to meet Zeke's accusing glare.

"Do you even have a plan in place?" Zeke pushed. "Where are you even keeping it anyway? I hope it's nowhere too warm."

Rhett's head whipped back in Zeke's direction.

"*Dude.* Tell me you don't have it someplace warm," Zeke said. "Please."

"Well, where else was I supposed to put it?" Rhett snapped. "You were trying to wrestle it from me like we were kids again."

"Hunh," I said, while Cole stiffened in interest

next to me. Tiger's eyes fluttered open before they closed again.

"Where is it?" Zeke insisted. When Rhett didn't answer right away, he barked, "Where, Rhett? *Where*?"

"Someplace safe. And I'm certainly not about to tell you where it is. You'll just steal it again."

"You're the one who stole it from me in the first place!"

"We can disagree about this all day long," Rhett said, but I was busy sweeping my eyes up and down his body trying to figure out where he could possibly be hiding an egg of any sort.

When he came through the portal, Uncle Tucker's magic dressed him in jeans that molded to his muscles and tight behind, and a sky-blue button-down shirt that hugged his straining biceps. He'd rolled up the sleeves of his shirt, exposing corded forearms wrapped in tattoos, sweeping shapes I couldn't quite make out unless I got him naked—from the waist up, anyhow.

I couldn't pick out a single place for him to hide any contraband.

A gentle finger beneath my jaw turned my head in Cole's direction.

"You're staring at the man's junk."

"I am not," I said, though I might've been. Just to be thorough. I was the sheriff after all. I had a duty to defend all Denners from ... eggs.

I swallowed a guilty smile and turned it coy. "Don't be jealous, baby. I'm just doin' my job. I have no earthly idea where he might be hiding whatever he's got."

Tiger chuffed and twitched his left whiskers, telling me I wasn't being subtle enough. And while I wasn't sure I wanted to be Missus Cole Bert, he was a fine man who deserved a good woman.

I just wasn't sure that's what I was, as I couldn't quite stop my attention from drifting over to Zeke.

He was dressed in similar fashion to Rhett, though wearing his cowboy hat, as Rhett's Stetson rested on the mattress behind him. Rhett's muscles were more developed, and the man appeared to have a significant amount of power simmering inside him. Zeke, however, seemed to spark with magic. Despite the lean frame of an athlete, who probably possessed impressive speed and agility, he was as imposing as Rhett.

Zeke's jeans also hugged muscles—pronounced and delicious. His blue eyes caught mine and I startled.

His sudden wicked smile said *caughtcha*. I

hurriedly pointed my eyes back at Rhett. Even afterward, the heat of Zeke's stare remained on my face, until he said, "Well, *Rhett*, where's the egg? Or should I have our friendly neighborhood sheriff strip search you? She looks willing."

"Hey," Cole snapped. "That's my girlfriend you're talking about. You'd better mind your tongue if you don't want a beatdown. I'll tan your hide and trade it to the taxidermist before you can blink twice."

Traitor's Den didn't actually have a taxidermist. Most of us were animal lovers, and those of us who weren't were actually animals—or magical creatures, as they largely preferred to be called.

"Don't mind him," Rhett told Cole. "He's used to bossing around his sex slaves."

Zeke sucked in a breath so fast he wheezed. "*Sex slaves*. For the last time, I don't have slaves, and if you say I do one more time I'm going to beat your ass so hard it'll shoot out your nose."

"He's already startin' to sound like a Denner," I told Cole, to relieve some of the tension in the air. But Cole didn't crack a smile.

"Besides," Zeke continued, face so close to Rhett's their noses almost touched. "I don't need to coerce the ladies to have sex with me. They come begging."

I grimaced. And here I'd thought Rhett was the full-of-himself asswipe. Seemed that was no longer an exclusive title.

"They beg because they know what I can do for them," Zeke added. "They know I'll kiss and lick and fulfill their every need, to their complete satisfaction, until they barely remember their names." He glanced at me and purred, "And that's a promise."

Cole was out of his seat so fast that his chair would've toppled over had I not caught it.

But Zeke ignored him. Even when Cole tried to get up in his business, he held up a hand, and kept his attention on Rhett.

Now, Cole might not be as big and muscled and ferocious-looking as Rhett, but Cole was one of the best catches in all of Traitor's Den. He was the very definition of tall, handsome, and gentlemanly. And he was strong too.

"Where's the egg?" Zeke pressed.

Rhett just stared back at him.

"Where. Is. The. Egg?"

Rhett laughed. "You sure it's not shoved up your ass? You know, to account for your charming personality?"

Zeke hissed. Rhett snarled. Cole growled. Tiger stretched and stood.

I whipped up and out of my chair. "That's enough. You're all bein' assholes. Every single one of you."

When Cole's mouth drooped, I marched over to pat him on the back. "Okay. Maybe not you. But definitely them."

I glared at our most recent residents. They stared each other down, not even bothering to look at me.

"I said, *enough* already," I told Zeke. "Rhett's in the clink for disturbin' the peace. Do you wanna join him? There's an empty cell with your name on it, just *beggin'* to be filled."

I'd meant to rib him, but the way I said it only sent my thoughts racing toward what Zeke might do to women to make them beg for more.

Feeling Cole's eyes on me like an unwarranted scarlet letter, I planted my hands on my hips. "I've had enough, boys. You start behavin' right this second, or I'll make you. And trust me, I have my ways, don't doubt that."

The furious set of Zeke's face softened. Even Rhett looked at me, considering.

I did my best to ignore the way three fine men were all checking me out.

I was the freaking sheriff. And I was on duty, even if it was after hours.

"Good," I said, as if they'd all decided to behave due to my command. "Now, where the hell is this egg? And what the dickens is inside it?"

Rhett sighed, reached into the waistband of his pants, rummaged around a bit, dipping into the area that should only have two balls, and emerged with an oval-shaped egg sized precisely to match a human testicle.

I breathed out in relief, unaware of how tense I'd been. An egg that small couldn't possibly be all that problematic.

"And what's growing inside it?" I asked, while Zeke muttered under his breath, "Absolutely disgusting."

"I'm not tellin' y—" Rhett started.

Zeke interrupted. "It's a dragon egg."

"A ... dragon egg," I repeated a bit numbly.

"Yes," Zeke said while Rhett growled in disapproval.

"*A dragon egg*. Meaning, the two of you idjits brought a *dragon* into Traitor's Den? A town that houses three-hundred-sixty-nine residents? A town that *no one can leave*?"

"Looks like," Zeke said.

"Damn." Blindly, I reached a hand out to scratch behind Tiger's ears and swallowed. "And how long do we have before ... you know?"

"We have a fire-breathing beast on our hands?" Zeke said.

I nodded, pulling my hat from my head with my other hand to shake out my hair, see if it helped me think better. This was something I had definitely not anticipated when I agreed to be sheriff.

"Well?" I prompted when neither man answered me. "How long?"

Rhett shook the bars but they didn't rattle. "We don't know."

"You don't know," I deadpanned.

"Nope. Didn't know there was a portal in the middle of a creek, ya know. It's not like I wanted to come here. I just dove in, trying to get away from this asshole."

"We're bound to have less time after all that ... incubating Rhett did." Zeke pointed a meaningful look at Rhett's crotch. As a sheriff, it was my duty to check out the region. When I'd duteously studied the sizable bulge there, I ran a hand through my hair, probably getting some of Tiger's fur in it. But I had bigger problems now, clearly.

"Okay. We'll figure it out. Somehow. I need a drink."

"I could use a drink too," Rhett said.

"Then you shoulda behaved when you got here."

Just as I was about to ask Tiger if he'd keep an eye on them while I went to down a Moon Mixer, or maybe even a Sirens on the Rocks—the situation definitely called for it—the door opened so forcefully that it slammed against the wall.

In walked Birdie, all smiles. "Hey, Loretta." Her eyes swept the scene, squinting. "What's goin' on? I heard we had some new guys…"

Her eyes grew as she took in the newcomers. Then she whistled. "Wow-eee. Guess they were worth the wait."

I grimaced. "You'll change your mind once you hang around them for a while."

"Hmm. We'll see. So, what'd I miss?"

"The bell clanging didn't wake you?"

"Un-unh. You know me. I sleep like the dead."

At least that was one constant fact in a world of sudden unknowns. Sighing, I wrapped my arm around her back, starting to lead her out. "Come on, join Cole and me for a drink. We'll catch you up."

"Hmmm," she hummed again, looking over her shoulder. "Maybe I should stay, watch over them."

"Tiger's got it. Right, Tiger?"

He chuffed importantly. Zeke gave him a wary look, proving he was smarter than Rhett, who snarled.

"Let's go," I tried again. "You'll need a drink for this one. And if you don't, I think better when I'm drunk."

That part wasn't precisely fact, but it sounded good. I led my best friend and boyfriend out of the office, breathing more freely once the dark of night swept over us. The air was hot and stifling, but I was away from the idjits who'd done nothing but land problems at my feet since their arrival.

Oh, and a *dragon's* egg. How could I forget?

The day was shaping up to be a real doozy. And I'd thought the worst of it would be dealing with Ollie and Leroy and a cock, who was more ladies' man than they were.

How wrong I'd been...

CHAPTER 7

*Rhett's Goods Are a Big Concern*

Birdie was my opposite in most ways, but not in the ways that mattered most. Her hair was strawberry blond and currently cut to her chin. She was short; I was more or less tall. I had the kind of curves that most men loved, while she was straight as a board.

Her laugh was infectious, and her eyes sparkled with mischief. She'd had more boyfriends than I had. I'd always had the one: Cole.

Birdie and Cole had been the first younger residents to arrive in Traitor's Den, bringing the median age of Denners down by a dozen points all on their own. I'd been thirteen then, and desperate to interact with others my own age. I'd latched on to Birdie and Cole out of desperation more than interests in common. Desperation had morphed into real love for the two of them somewhere along the way.

Birdie was currently leaning on her elbows at our usual table, deep into her second Fruity Tooty, a drink I'd long suspected Sharmayne developed just for her. It was bright, sparkly, loud, sweet, and fizzy —just like she was.

"Man." She shook her head, making her hair bounce around her face, as she'd done half a dozen times already. "Can't believe the one time I decide to take an afternoon snooze, shit goes to hell in a fancy handbasket."

I snorted. "Yeah, right. You forget how well we know you."

Cole sat next to me, his chair pulled close enough that he could sling his arm around the back of mine. "You wouldn't hit a lick at a snake, Birdie. It'd slither right up to you and bite ya hard before you even bothered to move, and you know it."

Birdie shrugged, never one to be overly concerned with what others thought of her. "Either way, seems like I missed out this time."

She pouted, and even that somehow seemed like a jovial expression, before she whisked it away. Her eyes widened and her smile grew. "Finally. Fresh meat. Mmm-mmmm." She sipped at her Fruity

Tooty before upending the glass, the motley colors of a fruit bowl sliding into her mouth.

Cole tsked. "Birdie, you can't objectify us men like that. It's not right."

She snorted and slammed her glass on the table loudly enough for Sharmayne to notice. The bar matron raised an eyebrow, Birdie nodded, and Sharmayne began preparing a third Fruity Tooty. At this rate, Birdie was going to get drunk before I did.

"I'm not objectifying *you*, Cole," Birdie said. "I never objectify you. You're Loretta's. I've known that since I first caught ya both neckin' in the back of the horse stalls."

"He's not *mine*," I grumbled.

"That's biased objectifyin'," Cole said. "If you objectify all the other men, you should objectify me too."

Birdie laughed, throwing her head back with her mirth. "I'm not objectifyin' everybody, Cole. Don't be daft. I'm not checkin' out our fine mayor or Hank Henry or Lonnie, bless 'im. I'm just objectifyin' those two fine hunks of fresh meat."

Sharmayne's skirts bustled behind us and she slid a new drink in front of Birdie, and another in front of Cole and me, winking at me. "Figured you'd want another."

"Thanks, Shar. Sure do."

"Them boys are troublemakers, no doubt about it. That Rhett could start an argument in an empty house, that he could."

"Yeah," I said on a sigh. "That's what I'm afraid of."

Birdie turned in her seat to face Sharmayne, grinning. "Guess what?"

"What?"

"Can ya keep a secret?"

No, no, Sharmayne most certainly could not. I cupped my Moon Mixer in both palms and narrowed my eyes at Birdie, focusing on shooting lasers at her. The hot burning kind she couldn't help but notice.

She didn't even glance my way.

"'Course I can keep a secret, honey bun." Sharmayne took a seat in the empty chair at our table. "You know me."

Yep, sure did. I glared at Birdie some more. She waved me off.

"Rhett brought some contraband with him from the other side."

I sucked in a breath. "Birdie, that's sheriff business."

Finally, she looked my way. "Don't worry. I'm

not gonna divulge *what* he brought, 'cause that's 'sheriff business.'" And she actually used air quotes. "But surely we can share a little tasty morsel with Shar. She treats us right. We wanna treat her right too, don't we?"

In that, Birdie might be right. It paid a hundred times over to allow Sharmayne in on exclusive gossip, even if it was incomplete. It wouldn't be exclusive for long—not after she rose from our table and sped to the next patron to share the news—but we'd be in her good graces for a long while.

Nodding, I forced a smile. Birdie might have a decent idea here, but she'd been as subtle as a herd of stampeding mustangs, and just as considerate.

"Tell her," I finally said.

Sharmayne leaned on the table, eyes dancing. A customer called for her; she steadfastly ignored them. "What's the news?" She licked her lips.

Birdie leaned toward her conspiratorially. "You know Rhett, the new guy?"

Sharmayne licked her lips again.

"Well, he smuggled in … something … purty crazy—really *nuts*, one might even say. And our girl Loretta will tell us more about what it is when it stops bein' sheriff-only business. But till then, you're the first to know."

"Yeah?" Sharmayne was leaning so far onto the table that her bosom was pushed up like a choker around the base of her throat. Cole averted his eyes from the voluminous swells like the gentleman he was.

Birdie leaned farther so she could whisper, though she never did anything truly quietly. The natural din in the saloon would cover up her complete inability to use an inside voice.

"He smuggled in the goods ... in his goods." Then Birdie winked once, twice, and a third time for good measure.

"In his *goods*?" Sharmayne's plucked eyebrows arched precariously. "You mean..."

Birdie grinned. "Oh yes, that's exactly what I mean." I groaned at her theatrics, because if not I'd laugh, and I didn't want to encourage her.

"In his..." Sharmayne stopped to look around us. More than one of her patrons had spotted the scene and were watching us. Again, the bar matron licked her lips as if she could lap up the juicy morsels. "In his ... pants ... ya mean?"

Cole groaned. "Seriously, ladies? What happened to decorum and modesty?"

As one, we three women stared at him and barked out a laugh.

"You forget," Sharmayne asked, "that we gotta survive this wild prison we've been thrown in? If we had to be all modest and prissy, then we'd die of boredom long before we find a way to escape this place."

"Too right, Shar," Birdie said. "Gotta get our kicks wherever we can." Then she looked from me to Cole and back again.

"At least the two of you get to ... entertain each other."

"Girl," I said, "you've just about dated every guy here at least once."

"Yeah, and what's that tell you? You snagged the best one."

Cole's chest puffed out like a damn monkey while I swallowed the mother of all groans. Birdie wasn't wrong. Cole was awesome. He was sweet and kind and respectful. He was even fun and sexy. I realized full and well how lucky I was. But I hadn't yet been able to make my heart feel something it didn't. I loved him, yes. Did I *love* him and want to wake up next to him every day for the rest of my life?

Yeah, that was the problem. I didn't think I did.

"Where'd she go?" Sharmayne asked Birdie under her breath, though Sharmayne whispered just about as well as Birdie, eyeing me as she did.

I blinked at them, clearing the familiar worry. "I'm here," I said and smiled a bit. "Just tired. It's been a long day, and it's far from over."

Cole scooted his chair all the way against mine, so that our legs pressed against each other. One hand squeezed my shoulder, the other rubbed my bare thigh. His lips tickled my ear as he murmured, "I got you, babe. Whatever you need, I'm here for you."

See? Sweet as one of Ashlyn Bates' teatime cakes, the ones dripping with her signature icing.

I forced another smile, dread washing through me. Cole had shot through the portal with his father at the age of sixteen. He was twenty-five now. He'd been trying to tie me down for nine years. I felt the imagined lasso tighten around my neck as if it were made of real rope.

Hiding my face behind my drink, I took a sip, then another, and finally downed the whole thing.

"Anything else you can tell me?" Sharmayne asked hungrily, though she'd leaned back in her chair.

"No." I stood, suddenly ready to get out of there. "And if you'll all pardon me, I gotta get back to it. The boys indeed brought trouble with them, big trouble, and the sooner I get to figurin' it out, the better off we'll all be."

Cole upended his beer, but I put a steadying

hand on his shoulder. "You stay here. Keep Birdie company. I've got this."

"I don't like how they look at you."

I was busy trying to come up with what to say when Birdie waved a hand in front of her, smirking. "Nothin' you can do about it, Cole. Our girl here is smokin' hot goods. You know that. That's why you tap that as often as you can."

"Birdie," I chastised—as if it'd do any good. Surely by now I knew better, but I couldn't seem to get myself to stop trying.

"I'm just speakin' the obvious. You're a looker, so men can't help but look. Hell, you even give Coby Rae whiplash, and she knows she don't have a chance in hell with you since you're so fond of the low hangin' fruit."

Birdie winked furiously at me.

"That's not what that means, you know," I said.

"Doesn't it mean whatever I want it to mean? I bend words to my will like a freaking word-flapping-smith. Like I was made to speak and shit."

I stared at her until the laughter bubbled up and I couldn't contain it. "Those curse words lose a lot of luster without being able to use the real F-bomb."

"Stupid freaking rule," she and I said together,

and I laughed again, before adding, "You're ridiculous, you know that, right?"

"You say ridiculous, I say glorious." She shrugged. "Same thing, isn't it?"

I snorted a laugh. "Yes. Definitely."

Cole went to rise, and I shook my head. "For real, stay." Then I smiled again to soften the request. "I'll catch up with you later. I need to focus now on the little problem of Rhett's *goods*."

Only Rhett's goods weren't at all minor, and I meant both the dragon egg and the smuggler's packaging.

"Ope." Sharmayne patted the table and got up too, looking toward the stairs at the back of the saloon. "Kiki's ready. Thanks for the tidbit, y'all." She smacked her lips like what Birdie had told her was delicious, then hollered, "Who's waitin' for a turn with Kiki?"

Kiki the koala was at the top of the staircase, hugging a fancy, carved balustrade.

Several hands shot up amid the sea of people huddled over drinks. Sharmayne, wielding her power with evident satisfaction, pointed at Dewey Gunner.

"I think you need her lovin' most right now. But don't take too long. Others be waitin'."

"Thank ya kindly, Shar," he said right away,

sliding out of his seat and skedaddling up the stairs, an extra pep in his step already. Kiki took his hand and led him to one of the rooms.

Uncle Tucker was apparently a bit of a perv, or maybe he was just sleazy. Either way, he'd imagined a whorehouse into the second level of Sharmayne's Den, complete with gaudy frilly curtains and velvet scarlet bedding.

Since none of us women were fond of selling our bodies, and we'd take turns kicking the ass of any man who dared suggest it, we had no use for the upstairs bedrooms except as temporary lodging for new arrivals.

But when Kiki had ambled through the pocket portal like she was out for an easy breezy afternoon stroll, she'd taken over the upstairs. Her cuddles were legendary. Singlehandedly, she was responsible for the elevated happy levels of Denners. When someone was down, Doc Janie Holloway's first prescription was snuggle-time with Kiki.

She was made for it. Sweeter than anything in Emmaline Bay's Candy and Confectionary Shop, and warm and cozy with the softest fur I'd ever felt, Kiki was the blessing that kept on giving.

I was half tempted to put my name in line to get a turn with her. A hug from her washed away all worries better than a dunk in the cold water of the river.

Before Cole, Birdie, or Sharmayne could turn their attention back to me, I slipped out of the saloon, crossed the dusty street to my office, and tugged the door open with a rip-off-the-bandage-fast mentality.

Which meant Tiger wasn't expecting me.

There might be a man somewhere inside Tiger, but the longer he was stuck in his shifter form, the less of that man was left. I could see it in his eyes. He was almost all tiger now.

He should have heard and scented me coming. He should've been alert and sharp and possibly growling. Instead of allowing Rhett, of all people, to put his hands on him.

There, next to Rhett's cell, Tiger was sprawled on his back, balls hanging out, while Rhett gave his belly a vigorous rubdown. Tiger was purring, eyes shut, and didn't even flinch when I let the door slam behind me.

"What the hell have you done to Tiger?" I whipped out, then I growled. "You make my ass itch."

"I'm happy to scratch it next," Rhett said, smooth as silk, though much less refined.

I pointed my glare at Zeke next, since Tiger *still* hadn't opened his eyes.

"You were supposed to watch him," I accused, though I hadn't exactly asked him to, and he was more or less a prisoner himself—at the very least, he was a person of interest, even if I hadn't informed him so.

Zeke leaned back into the bars of the neighboring cell, where he sat on the floor against them, long legs kicked out in front of him. "I didn't realize I was supposed to keep him from being friendly for once."

"This isn't friendly," I snapped. "This is encroachment." It really wasn't, not at all, but the word slipped out, and I wasn't one to back down from a mistake—I was a Denner, after all, more than anybody.

I stomped over to Rhett's cell. "You stop that right now."

He smiled up at me lazily, *sexily*, and I wanted to reach between the bars of his cell to throttle him.

"Don't go throwing a hissy fit, now," he drawled, as if he'd already lived in Traitor's Den for a decade. "I was just being neighborly."

"Well you keep your neighborly hands to yourself. He's a man, not a pet."

I shot eye daggers at him, wholly unconcerned by the fact that I all but considered Tiger *my* pet. After more than ten years with him at my side, I loved him as much as I loved Cole, Birdie, my parents, and Jolene.

I felt my eyes heat to temperatures that might actually emit lasers, and Rhett finally pulled his hands back through the bars.

"Mind you keep them there," I said, "or I'll chop them off at the wrists. You'll have nubs for the rest of your days."

"No, I won't, but I'd still rather you not try."

Tiger opened one eye to study me, and I huffed. "Right, how could I forget? You're a shifter of some sort. You've got powers. Whoopty-freaking-fruit-cake-doo."

Then, because I could tell I was being about as mature as Birdie when she got stinking drunk, I whirled on the heel of my boot and stomped out into the night, letting the door fall shut loudly behind me once more.

If Tiger wanted to be a traitor, he could bloody well have them.

I bypassed the saloon and marched all the way home, where I didn't even pop in to say hi to my parents in the main house.

My studio was in the back. I slid inside silently and slumped to the floor, leaning against the door, trying my darnedest not to examine why I was acting like puberty was still messing with my hormones.

Tiger and I were pals long before I started caring about stupid, sexy men who did their best to mess up everything.

Tiger couldn't have the newbies—and they definitely couldn't have him.

## CHAPTER 8
## *Strawberry Shortcake Trumps a Handlebar Mustache*

It didn't take long to figure out what was bothering me. How could it, when I'd been moping and moaning about the same thing since I turned eighteen?

I ripped my Stetson off my head and flung it across the open single space that served as sitting area, bedroom, and kitchen. The only room segregated from the rest was the lav, with its simple toilet, bathtub, and sink. Uncle Tucker had thankfully not seen to punish my dad with a lack of indoor plumbing.

My hat landed upside down at the foot of my bed, right plumb in the middle of a dust bunny that told me both that I needed to sweep and that my mom hadn't been inside in a long while. I loved living behind the house I grew up in since my mom cooked like a goddess and I had no desire to learn until I needed to, but I had to continually remind her—and sometimes my dad, too—that I was no longer a child.

Sighing heavily, I picked myself off from the floor, dusted my seat, patted Big Bertha and Big Wilma reassuringly, and clonked over to rescue my hat with leaden steps. Here, in the privacy of my room, I could allow myself to wallow. It was the only place I could.

Adjusting the shiny brass sheriff's badge on my belt, I did my best not to feel it as a weight far heavier than it actually was.

So what if a dragon's egg had shown up in town? And so what if I was literally the only person in the entirety of Traitor's Den who didn't have some sort of magic to help solve the problem that landed right in my lap like a heaping, steaming load of cow manure?

Even Emmaline, whose skills extended only to the art of confectionary, and Sharmayne, whose powers were limited to crafting spectacular booze, had more magic than I did. Even Kiki, who still hadn't revealed her powers, and Henrietta Hammer, who kept the exact nature of her magic carefully guarded, had to have more of it than I did.

Every single resident of Traitor's Den had to have magic. It was a must. If not, they wouldn't have been able to see the pocket portal from the other side, much less travel through it.

Yet here *I* was. Stuck with two morons who'd brought through a dragon's egg to the one place in the entire world where they *really* shouldn't have.

And now Tiger was on their side. My one true friend, who was even more steadfast than Birdie or Cole, and who was far quieter, demanding nothing of me I wasn't ready to give.

Suddenly anxious to get back out there before I could drown myself in unbecoming self-pity, I stepped onto my small porch, put my hat back on, and quietly pulled the door shut behind me.

Tiptoeing past my parents' house, I thought I was in the clear until I heard the front door open behind me.

"Loretta Maybelle?" my momma asked suspiciously, as if it would be anyone else.

I held in a groan, mostly because she didn't deserve that from me, no matter what kind of mood I was in. Before I spun, I made sure to clear my face of all signs of the turbulence raging inside me.

She gasped, running out onto the porch, her hand to her chest amid her loose flowing locks that looked glamorous amid the surrounding parched desert. She wore form-fitting jeans, a low-cut button-down shirt patterned with dainty flowers. From what my parents told me, my mom was the original sexpot, and my dad was still proud that he was the one to snag her and make her his. They were obnoxiously cute together.

"Levi," she called back into the house. "Come quick. Somethin's wrong."

"Momma..." I started, but didn't get far.

She raced down the steps, hands already outstretched toward me. "Loretta Maybelle, don't even start with me. I'm your momma."

"I know."

"That means *I know* when something's goin' on with my baby girl."

"I'm not a baby anymore," I said, but allowed her to pull me into an embrace. I grunted a complaint even as I tucked my face in her shoulder.

Her hugs were as good as Kiki's, and just as healing.

My dad came rushing out of the house, tugging on one of his boots as he ran, hair in disarray.

I couldn't help but smile. Looking up at him from over my mom's arms, I asked, "You been nappin', Daddy?"

He scoffed, then frowned, hurriedly running both hands through his thick dark hair, though it never quite stayed where he put it. "I don't nap, honey, you know that."

My mom chuckled softly into my hair, the familiar sound comforting me in ways I hadn't realized I needed.

"Your daddy hasn't napped in his entire life, honey," she said. "You know that." But her eyes glittered with her own brand of mischief.

Levi scowled, but palmed my mom on the ass as he rounded her to me.

"Ew. Daddy," I whined, for like the millionth time. "I get that you two are in love, okay? No need to do that stuff in front of me."

My mom giggled. "Oh, sweetie, you should be glad we still have fun together. Not everyone makes it through twenty-two years of marriage with this much spark between them."

"Spark. Yuck." It truly was sickeningly cute.

My dad joined in, turning the embrace into a three-way hug. "What's going on, sweets? Why you sad and blue?"

"I'm not sad," I attempted.

"Un-huh," they both said in unison.

Dammit, they knew me too well.

"And where's Tiger?" my mom asked. "He never misses a chance to have my cookin'."

I turned my face to the side, hoping to avoid both of their eyes on me. "Tiger stayed at the jail. He's watching the new guys for me."

"I see," my dad said, as if he really might.

"And where are Cole and Birdie?" my mom followed up.

"At Sharmayne's."

"'Cause you asked them to stay behind?" my mom asked softly.

*Flatlined funnel cake!* They were reading me like a damn book.

"Mmm-hmmm." Then I tried to disengage.

They only hugged me tighter, before my mom wrapped an arm around me and steered me inside. "Your daddy and I were just about to sit down to a nice dinner. You join us now, darlin'."

I didn't bother refusing. It never did me much good, and besides, the smells alone were making my mouth water. Tiger was going to be bummed he missed out.

I allowed her to steer me into my usual seat while she plopped still-steaming bread on the table alongside her signature lentil stew, topped with sliced chives, chili hot sauce, and sour cream from one of the neighbors.

She poured me a glass of water. "Now, honey, tell us what's got your knickers in a knot. It's not the magic thing again, is it? You know your powers will show up when they're good and ready."

"It's not about my magic," I answered right away, unwilling to have another conversation about it and unbothered by the lie that would keep me from it. The whole truth and nothing but the truth was for patient people and martyrs. I was neither.

"Then what's this about, sweet pea?" my dad asked.

I sighed loudly, but then took my first bite of stew, followed by a mouthful of bread so hot it almost burned my mouth. Suddenly I didn't mind telling them what had happened since they left the saloon and returned home. My dad had been the unofficial sheriff until I'd come of age and assumed the role, and my mom had done as much policing as he had.

After half a loaf of bread with fresh butter, and two servings of stew, I'd caught them up and felt miles better.

My dad pushed back his chair and folded his hands

over his belly, which he occasionally rubbed, reminding me that he turned into a bear at will. My mom placed a plate of warm bread in front of him with a full pot of honey, and he smacked a kiss on her lips and patted her ass—again. I rolled my eyes but didn't say a thing. They'd been this way as long as I could remember.

"Did they say where they got this dragon egg from?" my mom asked as she re-took her seat.

"Nope," I said, realizing only then that I should have pressed for the answer to this question more forcefully. I was the sheriff, but it wasn't like anyone had trained me, not even my dad. I'd learned by being thrown in the fire, and so far the most dangerous situation I'd had to deal with was when Lonnie ate a batch of bad beans and proceeded to spread his rotten flatulence all over town, half suffocating the lot of us. I'd had the pleasant job of explaining to him how he was making the whole place flammable. One flick of a match and we'd all go up in smoke—or it felt that way anyhow.

"Did they say what kind of dragon's gonna hatch?" my dad asked.

"Nope, but they didn't know *when* it would hatch, so I don't think they know what kind it is either." Of course, that was a big, huge, ginormous assumption. I started a mental list of questions to ask them, hoping I'd keep track of them despite the two Moon Mixers I'd downed.

"Those boys are bad business, honey," my dad said. "You'd best stay clear of them. Want me to come help you handle them?"

"No," I started to say when Momma swatted his arm across the table, telling him, "You just don't like 'em 'cause you caught them checkin' out our Loretta Maybelle."

He grunted. "I didn't just catch 'em, they wouldn't stop with all their staring. They're egg-suckin' dawgs, both of them!"

Momma shrugged, and went on like I wasn't there with them, listening to every word. "Our daughter's a real beauty, babe. You can't fault them for appreciatin' her."

"Of course I can. She's *my* daughter."

"Every single man in town would have a go at her if she didn't have Cole, and a few married ones too, like our fine mayor."

I felt my face screw up in disgust. Mayor Reginald Roone had more hair on his chest than his head, and he liked to display the dark mass of it and the trio of gold chains hung low on his neck by leaving his shirts unbuttoned damn near to his bellybutton. He sported a handlebar mustache he twisted up at the ends and routinely licked to keep tamed.

"I'm glad I was finished eating or that would've made me lose my appetite," I announced.

"Does that mean you don't want a slice of my famous strawberry shortcake?" my mom asked, knowing full well I would never turn down a dessert that delicious, no matter what the two of them were going on about.

She grinned knowingly, stood, and began gathering plates, fresh utensils, and of course, the best cake ever made. "Jony brought over some strawberries, fresh picked, and let me tell you, they are dee-licious."

Jony was Momma's best friend and only slightly better behaved than mine.

When Momma turned to set the strawberry shortcake on the dining table, she startled at the fierce look I was giving her.

"Honey, I was gonna save some for you, promise."

"Aha," I said triumphantly. "So you knew I'd be bummed to miss out!"

"'Course I did. I'm your momma. I know everything about you."

I took a moment to secretly hope she didn't

know *everything*. Cole had a roommate, so we spent most of our long, sweaty nights at my place.

Within earshot of my parents.

I cleared my throat and began to say something else—anything else—when we all froze.

The bell clanged again.

Yes, *the* bell. *Again*. Twice in one day.

My parents' hound dog, Butch, bayed long and loud.

I was on my feet with one hand on the door, strawberry shortcake forgotten, when my dad called out, "Take Bear, since you don't have Jolene. He's out behind the house, grazin'."

I hesitated only until the bell clanged again. Bear was my dad's four-year-old stallion. He was a spitfire, fast as a whip.

As if reading my mind, my dad added, "Is Jolene out by your office?"

"Yeah, in front of Sharmayne's."

"I'll get 'er and bring her to you. Now go."

After that, I was off like a shot. I didn't even bother taking the time to saddle up Bear. I leapt onto him—and he took off.

It was like he knew what the bell meant too.

His hooves pounded across alleyways and streets, turning on a dime to weave across town, until we merged onto Main Street, joining up with a string of Denners, all headed in the same direction.

As if we were in a race, Bear whinnied and *charged*.

All I focused on was holding on.

## CHAPTER 9
## Mind Where You Stick Your Hands and Other Pertinent Warnings

Bear skidded to a stop mere feet from Portal Platform, winning by the skin of his teeth the race only the horses had been interested in running. A dozen other steeds slid to abrupt stops right behind him, kicking up clouds of dirt, and immediately crowding the platform.

The very *empty* platform.

Scowling at the open air where the pocket portal usually formed, I patted my dad's stallion on the neck. He breathed loudly, his sides heaving, but he tossed his dark mane haughtily.

"You did a great job, Bear," I told the prideful creature, who managed to turn just about everything into a competition. He snorted, whinnied, and pawed the ground as if I'd just awarded him a first-place prize. Then he looked around us at the other horses, as if to ensure they were watching while he received praise.

I snorted a laugh, but couldn't help but indulge him. "You're so fast and sleek, like a lightnin' bolt. You're a real champ, Bear."

He jerked his head back and neighed—twice.

If my dad were here, he'd admonish me for spoiling him. It was a missed chance to point out to my dad how *he* pampered Bear worse than anybody. The stallion got more carrots and sugar cubes than any other in Traitor's Den.

A second batch of riders arrived, swirling the dust that had only just begun to settle.

Ace Steele leaned out from the viewing stand above us. "Will all y'all stop kickin' up so much blasted dirt already? I can't see a damn thing with all the fuss you're makin'."

No one said a thing, because if we did, it'd be to point out that Ace Steele was one Denner who'd been oddly misnamed when he came through the portal. Ace hadn't been dealt a winning hand in ways that any of us had noticed. He could see well only about as far as his arm reached out in front of his face, and refused to wear the glasses Doc Holloway prescribed him. Even more perplexing than not wanting to wear bottle-bottom spectacles was refusing to do the rounds across town, searching for a witch or wizard who might have just the right kind of magic to fix him up.

By nature, Denners in general were a suspicious sort. They kept the specs of their powers to themselves unless they were motivated otherwise, often by significant value in trade. But with nearing on four-hundred residents, all of them with magic—save me—chances were decent that Ace Steele could get sorted.

However, he was as stubborn as he was blind.

He couldn't see much about Portal Platform with or without the clouds of dust. But he *could* make out the bright, nearly blinding lights of the pocket portal whenever it opened well enough for him to ring the bell above his head.

"What happened, Ace?" I called up, dismounting as I did. "Nothin' came through this time?"

"Nope. Nothin' t'all. First time ever for that, and it happened on my watch."

From where I was standing, that wasn't something to brag about, especially since I'd already spotted something shiny beneath Portal Platform, just barely reflecting the soft moonlight overhead.

"'Kay," I hollered up at him. "Thanks, Ace." With the man, who hadn't aged a day over sixty since he arrived twenty years ago, a *thanks for nothing much* went unsaid more times than not.

Walking around the other side of the platform to avoid the crowd of antsy horses, I crouched to peek under the old planks, warped and showing signs of wood rot.

What had caught my eye turned out to be a small potion bottle made from a blood-red glass. And inside it, a piece of curled paper.

"Oooh," I said to myself while I slid a hand toward it, into the shadows beneath the platform. It must have shot through the portal, unbeknownst to the trusty, half-blind watchman on duty, bounced off the platform, and rolled beneath it.

I slid my arm a little farther until the tips of my fingers skimmed cold glass—

A sharp, sudden pain sliced through my hand.

I whipped back with a startled cry. Had the attack not surprised me, I would have remained silent, especially when a horde of Denners I didn't want up in my business milled nearby.

But then a hot, blazing fire raged up my forearm, quickly licking up toward my shoulder. My hand

and arm *burned*, as if I were holding my arm over an open flame—over the gaping fires of hell.

I cradled the arm limply against my stomach, trying to figure out what was going on. My eyes felt glazed; I kept blinking to clear the fog so I could make sense of what was happening.

I heard voices growing closer. When bodies crowded around me, blocking what little illumination the moon afforded, my ears started ringing, and I couldn't make sense of anything any of them were saying.

The fire spread to my chest, suddenly making it hard to breathe. I gasped, rubbing at it, sucking in open-mouthed inhales while I still could, hazily wondering if I wouldn't be able to do so for much longer.

Someone shouted—no, *several* someones shouted. Activity I couldn't quite follow bustled around me.

I'd been crouched before; now I was lying down. Then yanked upward, my head pulled onto someone's lap.

The bell rang out again, its pace frenzied.

"Is somethin' else comin' through?" I mumbled thickly over an unwieldy tongue, unsure whether my words would be understood or not. Regardless, if I received an answer, I didn't register it.

I hadn't noticed the lights of the portal flashing, but then I wasn't sure I would.

The bell still clanged while the fire spreading inside me settled to a roiling simmer—

Then it intensified anew, its heat punishing, causing me to arch my back and gasp, mouth wide, like a fish caught out of water.

I continued to struggle to pull my surroundings into focus, for the first time wondering if this was the day I would die.

To consider I'd die without ever seeing anything beyond the town I was born in wasn't new. But to think I'd end like this ... mere weeks before my twenty-third birthday ... I sure hadn't seen it coming.

The bell rang out as furiously as the fire that consumed me. It took over my chest, searing it as if pan-frying my heart.

I opened my mouth but whatever came out was surely garbled. I'd never claimed to be the most elegant or graceful, definitely not the most dainty or feminine, of the women in Traitor's Den. Surely I deserved a more dignified death than this though.

And Tiger ... I'd resented my friend for accepting a belly rub from an asshole. Who was I to deny him the pleasures of life wherever he could find them? He was a man trapped in the body of an animal.

For the first time, I felt as if I might truly understand Tiger's predicament. My body was beyond my control. The burn seeped into my stomach, I felt myself whimper, and bit down on my lip to keep the sounds inside.

Hands patted me down, then squeezed my hand. I screamed. I hadn't realized I'd do it, but I couldn't stop it from tumbling out.

My hand was squeezed again, so hard that tears rolled down my cheeks, and I began shaking from the shock.

But finally I recognized who it was. Glancing down, through a blur, I managed to make out the long gray hair and lean body of Janie Holloway, our one physician, who considered herself more witch doctor and shaman than the kind of doctors Momma told me about outside our town.

Doc Holloway was talking to me. I could tell more from the vibrations of her words than anything else. When she squeezed my hand a third time, making everything in my body clamp down to survive the pain, I guessed she'd been warning me of what was coming.

If I'd understood her, I might have finally been

able to make it past Uncle Tucker's rules against the F-bomb. The thoughts sparking through my mind were littered with the real deal.

The burning sting licked at my lower back, up and down my spine, slinking along to pool in my groin. The magnitude of my pain blossomed with so much ferocity that it mimicked the sudden explosion of pleasure. The sensation, however, was fleeting, and there was no relief such as what came with orgasm.

I panted, fervently wishing I could escape my body.

Doc pressed down on the flesh of my hand another time, where the burn was strongest, where it was unrelenting—and everything began to go black.

Happily, my panicked thoughts skipped toward the pull of oblivion, anxious to succumb to it—

An enraged, beastly bellow tugged me back to the here and now.

To the pain. To the motherfreaking *paaaaain*.

When an ordinary animal cry would begin to dip to an end, this one only gathered more momentum. It became louder, more ferocious, until it blew my hair back from my face, whipping like wind instead of sound. Until it slid me back several feet, dragging my body across dirt, scraping my bare lower back, legs, and arms. I winced at the brief sting that was the least of my problems.

The interminable roar overpowered the startled yelps that came from the others. It consumed every other sensation but my reaction to this animal outcry.

Finally, the burning began to ease, to pass, and I nearly whimpered in relief. With my wits beginning to return, I pressed my lips shut so I wouldn't let slip another sign of vulnerability.

As the only Denner without magic, and as the sheriff, I shouldn't reveal weaknesses.

Tonight, I'd exposed far too many of them.

The roar finally reached its crescendo. It blew my hat right off. Mine wasn't the only one, as others rolled along with it, like a collection of tumbleweeds.

But then ... the cry began to soften, and my hair fell back down to pool around my shoulders, the pain receding along with the roar, until nothing but a loud, echoing silence remained, temporarily obscuring the usual sounds of the desert—the skittering of animals, the occasional howling of coyotes, the scampering of diurnal creatures as they nested in anticipation of a night's rest.

My skin still stung, but nothing like it had

before. My thoughts crystallized into coherent, useful forms, and my eyes managed to focus.

Doc Holloway knelt over me, the back of my hand pressed to her mouth, where she sucked on my skin as if she were drinking through a straw. I would've asked her what the hell she was doing, but that wasn't the weirdest sight of them all.

Bobbie Sue stood at my feet with the small, delicate-looking red bottle in one hand, a matching cork stopper in the other. Her hair, usually falling around her shoulders in soft, bouncy curls, stood on end in every direction, straight as a rod, as if she'd jammed her fingers into a socket juiced up with Uncle Tucker's magic. Her eyebrows were singed and barely there, her eyes locked into wide, blinking shock—like an owl. Her shirt was tattered, her lacy bra peeking through everywhere, revealing reddened skin underneath—the same color as her face. It was as if she'd been struck by lightning after getting the worst sunburn of her life.

Ashton Blu approached her with the wariness of a man sneaking up on a rabid animal. Cautiously, he reached a hand to her arm. Extending a single index finger, he poked her and quickly yanked his hand back.

Red sparks erupted on her bare shoulder, making

him yelp as they jumped to him and raced up his finger.

Shaking out his hand, he studied her. "Get a stick, a long 'un," he ordered no one in particular, but a few Denners jumped to fulfill his wish. "It's like she's electrified. We gotta treat her like a heifer in a lightnin' storm."

Under normal circumstances, Bobbie Sue would've made Ashton pay for likening her to a cow, but all she did was blink and stare blankly ahead.

I groaned and tried to sit up, but Doc Holloway shook her head, muttering a *nah-ah* around sucking my hand. When she put it down to rest on my leg, she shook her head some more, her own long gray locks extra voluminous after the shock of standing too close to whatever had emerged from that tiny, innocent-looking bottle.

"Don't move yet, woman," Doc told me, removing her belt and wrapping it in a tourniquet above my elbow. "You got bit, and the poison nearly stopped your heart. Don't wanna get your heart pumpin' that venom through your veins any faster. I'm still workin' over here."

And by working, she meant sucking like she could be the sole worker in sleazy Uncle Tucker's whorehouse.

Ashton was handed two long sticks, and he armed himself with one in each hand. Carefully, as if Bobbie Sue were herself a lightning bolt, he inched toward her, then bopped her on the shoulder and leg with the sticks.

Bobbie Sue toppled. Like a felled tree, she was standing one moment, the next falling straight back like a board.

We were all too stunned to do much more than watch her crash to the ground, where she landed so hard she bounced, the bottle and stopper tumbling from her hands.

After she landed, Ashton tossed the sticks and raced to her side. Others followed, soon obstructing my view of the normally loud, upbeat woman who still hadn't so much as squeaked.

"She gonna … 'kay?" I mumbled at Doc. It was the best I could do.

Doc Holloway glanced over her shoulder at Bobbie Sue before looking back at me. "Can't know for certain, Loretta, but I think so. She didn't get the worst of it, you did."

That's when I noticed how clouded Doc's usually bright brown eyes were. How her brows were drawn low and she kept chewing on her lip.

Doc Holloway was composed in the face of every emergency. Calm under pressure. Zen as Kiki.

Only, she wasn't now. A storm brewed in those knowing eyes of hers.

"What happ'ed to me?" I slurred, feeling drunk with relief that the pain had finally subsided enough for me to think straight, if still woozy from the aftershock of enduring so much discomfort.

Doc made me wait while she sucked on the back of my hand some more, then turned it this way and that to examine it under the silver moonlight. "Better," she said under her breath to herself before she met my waiting stare.

"Best I can tell, Loretta, you got stung."

In my mind, I snorted and rolled my eyes. I didn't have the energy to do it outwardly. But, *duhhhhhhh*. Of course I got stung.

"You got bit by what looked mighty like a..." Doc paused to waggle her jaw some. "...a dragon?"

Her statement was more question than anything, but I couldn't exactly blame her. There were no dragons around that I could see, and I was fairly certain we'd notice one.

"A drag'n?" I repeated best I could.

She nodded, her hair a frizzy mess of a halo around

her. "Best I can tell, anyhow. It blasted the cork off the bottle and whipped out of it to take a chunk out of your hand. I didn't know dragons could inject venom with their bites, but your body's reactions taught me something new. That's fun," she said, but she looked so dazed that she probably wasn't fully registering what she was saying. "Then the dragon just disappeared... like."

Her eyes lost focus, and I realized she was no longer seeing me. "The dragon was a messenger," she announced in that eerie monotone voice she used when she was tapping into her magic—or perhaps simply her intuition; she'd never bothered to clarify the issue.

"Then what'd he say?" I asked, my words coming clearer now.

"What'd *she* say. That dragon was most definitely a female. They're meaner than a half-drowned cat out for revenge."

"Dandy," I managed around a swallow. If what I'd had was a taste of pissed-off she-dragon, I was gonna take a hard pass at seconds.

I waited, watching the doc while Denners bustled around downed Bobbie Sue and me. When she didn't add anything else, I pressed, "And her message? What was it?"

Doc turned to me, blinking as if she'd forgotten I

was even there for a hot second. It was her channeling-wisdom look, and it made my ass itch. Really, it made me itchy all over.

Last time she'd looked like this, she'd told me Lily White was gonna kick the bucket, something the old bird had promptly done the very next day.

"We don't need to wonder about the message," Doc said, back to her regular voice, and I dared relax a bit. "Her message is inside the bottle. All we need to do is read it."

Then someone called for Doc to come check on Bobbie Sue, and my mom, dad, Cole, and Birdie appeared at my side, out of breath from running. While they fretted, I could only think about the message, the bottle, and the she-dragon that had come flying out of it—before disappearing.

And the fact that Traitor's Den was now in possession of a *dragon's egg*.

If I allowed myself to believe that was a coincidence, I'd be no sheriff at all.

My ass was back to itchin'...

CHAPTER 10

## I'll Be Good and Other Lies

Ashton Blu was taking far longer than was reasonable to dislodge the scrap of paper from inside the bottle. His fingers were too thick to fit inside the narrow glass neck, but he refused to hand over the vessel to anyone else, insisting that the message was probably for him to read, since he and Bobbie Sue had been the ones to send a message through earlier. He entirely skirted over the fact that no one from the other side could have read that missive, since the portal had launched it back through to bonk him on the head.

From my position sprawled out on the ground and commanded by Momma not to "dare move a hair on your head yet, Loretta Maybelle," I noticed how Ashton's hands trembled.

Sure, from my angle I could also make out Bobbie Sue's boots right behind him, sticking straight up as if she were deader than a doorknob, and though she and Ashton Blu had been fast friends since they met, he wasn't paying her any mind.

But ... this was the very first time since the creation of our town that anything had come through to us, unbidden to boot. And Ashton had left behind a pregnant wife when he decided to explore where the portal that opened in the forest behind his house might lead.

"A pin," he snapped, then returned his tongue to its previous position, pressing against his upper lip in concentration. "A hairpin, a bobby pin. Somethin'. Anythin', so I can get in there."

When no one came running, he barked, "Now, people! We got us a message here. It could be the solution to everything."

Before even reading this message, I highly doubted it was the solution to *everything*. We had a long list of largely unsolvable problems here in Traitor's Den. Every new Denner to come through the portal only added to it.

In fact, I was growing more concerned by the second that the message wasn't going to be anything any of us wanted to hear.

I had no magic. Zippppp-o. And I'd never been prone to premonitions à la Doc Holloway either. But I was getting jittery when I should've been looser than a wet noodle. After that kind of pain, I should've been craving nothing more than a nice long nap to help me forget about all that had happened since Rhett and Zeke came barreling through the portal.

And yet, adrenaline was beginning to pump through me anew, the ministrations of my loved ones starting to annoy me. Trying not to be a dick about it, I waved away Momma and Daddy's fussing, then Cole's and Birdie's. Even Jolene hovered above me, her body appearing larger and more imposing from my perspective.

Henrietta Hammer rushed over to Ashton, pulling her hair out of its twist as she went. "Will this work, ya think?"

Without thanks, which was most unlike Ashton, who possessed as many gentlemanly manners as Cole, he snatched the fancy silver barrette from her outstretched hand.

She startled; he didn't even notice. I felt like making his excuses for him, but he'd do it later, once he realized how he'd behaved in his frenzy.

His tongue crept higher until it was all but up

one nostril as he dug the slimmest part of the barrette into the bottle, snagged the note, and ... slowly ... inched it out.

"Got it!" he exclaimed as if he were world champion of ... something. Ashton Blu was predictable in his mediocrity. He was a wizard, but not a great one. Mostly he used his magic to float around brooms, mops, buckets, sponges. He was a real stickler for keeping a clean house.

"Well," my mom said, "then stop standin' there being about as useful as a steering wheel on a mule. Read us the damn note, Ashton."

He hopped from foot to foot as if he'd piss his pants if he stopped. "Right, right." An infectious, albeit somewhat manic grin spread across his face. "Y'all, we got a note from the outside!" Once more, he thrust it into the air like a trophy, then hustled to unwind it before my mom got on his case again.

Even unrolled, the note was small enough to fit entirely in the palm of his hand. He stared at it, unblinking. Then he turned it around, upside down, and blinked at it. He tilted the note this way and that before finally turning it around to study its backside.

Momma rose in a huff and stalked over to him, snatching the paper from his hand. "Do ya mind tellin' us what it says before we all die of old age out here? You're slower than cream rising on buttermilk. For fart's sake..."

Momma studied the paper, rapidly turning it in every direction as Ashton had. "This is gibberish. What the hell is this?" She handed it off to my dad, who passed it on to Henrietta, who finally passed it off to Doc Holloway.

"Damn," Doc said. "No wonder we can't read it. These are some kinda runes."

"What kinda runes?" I asked, pushing up to my elbows.

"Take it easy. Please, honey," my dad said, and I nodded reassuringly, still waiting for Doc's answer. She had that eerie distant look on her face again, and I didn't think I was going to like what she said next.

"It's dragon runes," she announced in awe, opening her eyes again. "Wow. *Dragon runes*."

I knew I wasn't going to like it!

She looked at the note again, humming this time. "Yep. That's it. We're gonna need a talkin' dragon to read the message here, preferably a friendly one, so probably a male. Or I guess a dragon shifter would do too."

When Doc seemed oblivious to the disappointment making the night air as oppressive as the heat of high noon, I asked, "So, Doc, you happen to have a male dragon or one of them dragon shifters tucked up your sleeve you didn't tell us about? 'Cause far as I know, that leaves us up shit's creek without a paddle or a chance in hell of gettin' one."

"Can't've ... note. No. Note. Dragnooon rawr."

We all looked over in the general direction of Bobbie Sue.

Ace Steele looked down at her and said, "She's comin' to. Lookin' good."

Only Bobbie Sue had obviously *already* come to, and she wasn't sounding all that good.

Doc walked over to hand me the note, then busied her hands weaving her long hair into a braid. "Don't worry about Bobbie Sue. She's fine. Just got zapped by the dragon. She'll unfrazzle."

"Soon?" I asked hopefully.

Doc shrugged. "Who knows? Not like I've ever seen a dragon specter before, or whatever it was. That was some fine-ass dragon magic, that was."

Entirely unreassured, I asked, "If it wasn't a real dragon, then how'd it bite me like a snake?"

Another shrug. "Magic, I'm sure. A whole hell of a lot of it, too, I'd guess."

"Yeehaw. Just plumb dandy."

My mom was back at my side, patting my

shoulder in empty reassurance. It still helped. "Don't you worry, honey. We'll figure it out. We always do."

I wanted to believe her, I really did. But we'd never dealt with dragons, dragon shifters, or dragon eggs before.

I rubbed a hand over my face, feeling like I hadn't slept in years.

"It was mighty purty too," Doc continued. "The dragon magic. Bright reds and pinks, and the oranges, yellows, and blues of flames. It was like it was real, only not real. Like a hologram."

I'd never had occasion to witness a hologram since we didn't have them in Traitor's Den, but I followed well enough.

"The she-dragon shocked poor Bobbie Sue with its power, but since it wasn't a real dragon, her chances of recovery are decent."

Decent? Hadn't Doc just said Bobbie Sue would unscramble for sure?

I finally studied the note in my hands. The paper was tinged a watered-down red, and the ink was the color of fresh blood. The symbols covered the entire small page in tight, controlled script. But I didn't recognize a single shape amid the looping curves and slashing lines.

"Oh shit," I said before I properly registered what I was thinking.

"What?" my mom and dad both asked right away, and Cole scooted closer to me.

A vertical line creased the space between my mom's eyebrows, something I'd never seen. "Are you all right? Is it the venom again?" She whipped her head around. "Doc, what's goin' to happen with the venom? Is my daughter safe?"

"She'll be fine. But she needs to take it easy for a few days to make sure. Nothing that gets the blood pumpin', ya hear?" At that, Doc pinned me *and* Cole in a meaningful look.

I rolled my eyes so I wouldn't blush. We were consenting adults, dammit.

I hurried away from the topic. "I'll be good."

It was, of course, an empty promise. I tried very hard *not* to be good any more than necessary as a general rule. Misbehaving was so much more fun.

"I have a theory," I said, "but I want to test it out before I tell any of y'all." I pushed up to sitting, and Momma's eyes widened as if I were on fire all over again.

"I'm fine," I told her, though I wasn't sure I was. But I'd be fine. "I just need to try somethin' on my own. Then I'll let y'all know one way or another."

I stood and wobbled. In a heartbeat, Momma and Daddy were there, holding me from either side. Cole hovered around me like a mother hen. Birdie, however, who liked to join me in misbehaving on the regular, circled Jolene around for me.

"Birdie," Momma gasped. "You can't possibly expect her to ride. She can hardly stand up straight."

"She's been ridin' long as she's been walkin'," Birdie said. "And I've seen her ride when she couldn't stand from drink."

I frowned, wishing I could turn around to glare at her. Birdie was *not* helping things. But sudden movements were definitely a no-no. That much I could tell.

"How 'bout this?" Birdie tried again. "I'll ride with her to make sure she holds on."

When Momma's face was still scrunched into an accordion of concern, she added, "She's gotta get back to town somehow. She can't very well kick up and sleep out here. The coyotes'll get her and Ace'll be none the wiser."

"Hey," Ace said, but we ignored him. It was probably true.

"Fine," Momma finally said, as if it were up to her. *Consenting adult over here, remember?* But I knew she only did it because she loved me so much that she forgot I wasn't fragile as the porcelain teapot she had at home, glued back together a dozen times—with her magic.

"But we're riding right behind you," Daddy said.

"Damn straight we are," Momma added.

"I'm coming too," Cole chimed in.

I smiled tightly. "Fine." I glanced back at Bobbie Sue, who was sitting up now, then Doc. "She's all right for sure?"

"I promise," Doc said. "And I won't leave her side till she's walkin' and talkin' same as always."

I hoped Doc was up for a sleepover, then. Bobbie Sue still looked like she'd walked through a horde of ghosts.

I allowed my parents to help me up into the saddle behind Birdie—lucky she was slim so we'd both fit—and I wrapped my arms tightly around her tiny waist to reassure them. And when Jolene started off, she walked so slowly it'd take us at least an hour to get where we were going.

"Home?" Birdie asked over her shoulder.

"Nope."

She turned to glance at me. "Where, then? You're in no shape for a drink, no matter what you think. Your hair's a mess, you got scrapes and cuts all over, and there are holes in your shirt in all the right places, if you get my drift."

I always did, for better or for worse.

"We're not going to Sharmayne's. We're headed to the jail."

"The jail? Why? Haven't you had enough trouble from those two?" She paused. "Oh wait. Or are we going there 'cause you *want* some of their flavor of trouble to take your mind off things?"

I huffed impatiently. "I'm not going to the jail to jump either of the newbies. Honestly, Birdie…"

"What? They're hot as sin—both of 'em—and I know how hot you like your sin…"

There was no denying either of those points. Birdie was simply stating facts for once, no exaggeration. But—

"I'm with Cole, remember? I'd never do that to him. He deserves better."

Birdie was silent for a long while, which immediately made me suspicious.

I glanced behind us, confirming that my parents and Cole were riding far enough behind that they couldn't overhear. The stretches of desert we crossed were empty of everything but cactuses, tumbleweeds, and gnarled and twisting Juniper trees.

"What're you thinking?" I asked, wondering if I'd regret asking.

"You say Cole deserves better. But did you stop to think, maybe you deserve better than Cole?"

I gasped, definitely not expecting *that*. Birdie was Cole's number one fan.

"Cole's amazing," I told her. "He's respectful and kind, and he treats me like a queen. And he's sweet and handsome. He's—"

"He's definitely amazing, you and I both know that. But, Lo, you don't look at him the way he looks at you. You must've noticed by now."

I slumped forward, dropping my chin onto her shoulder until the up and down of Jolene's gait rattled my jaw too much.

"I know you mean to do right by him," Birdie said far more softly than usual, "but what about doing right by you?"

"I do love him," I said.

"I know you do. But you also love me and Jo here and Tiger and your crazy-ass, horn-dog parents."

I had nothing to say to that. She was right.

"There's love, and then there's *love*. The kind where you can barely stand to be around each other without ripping your clothes off and having at each other, right then and there. Don't you think you deserve that?"

Again, I said nothing.

"You do, Lo. Just because Cole landed in your lap and's been at your side ever since, doesn't mean he's perfect for you. People change."

I turned my head to the side, leaning it against her back, watching the flat landscape scroll by.

"You already know it, don't you?" she asked after a while. "It's why you keep shootin' him down when he asks you to marry him."

"He's just so good though, Bird. He's exactly what I should want." And then I registered the words I spoke.

Birdie was right. The truth was staring me straight in the face.

"I don't want to hurt him," I whispered so that she could barely hear me over Jolene's clip-clopping.

"You can't help that. But it'll be better for him in the long run. He deserves to be loved the way he loves you."

"I know he does. I want that for him."

We rode in silence for so long that even I was surprised when my secret worry bubbled up and out. "I don't want to lose him."

Birdie patted my arms looped around her waist,

mindful not to touch the angry red bite. "You won't ever lose him. First off, there's nowhere for him to go." She laughed, but the sound that usually brightened my heart failed to do so.

She sobered. "It might take him a while to get over it—over *you*—but he'll get there eventually. And when he does, he'll remember that we three are all great friends. He won't want to lose you either."

"It sucks," I mumbled.

"Yep. Sure does. But focus on the good points of breaking up with him."

"Such as?"

"New cock."

I slapped her on the back; all she did was chuckle.

"Don't bother denying it," she said. "I've seen you eyeing the two guys you've got locked up in your jail. So you can find them when you want them."

I didn't bother pointing out that Zeke wasn't even locked up, or any of the other nonsense she'd made up.

"There's nothing wrong with knowin' what you want. It just happens that's not Cole anymore. Don't feel bad about that. It's natural. Some people grow closer over time, like you and me. Some people grow apart. Ya can't force feelings."

I sighed, already dreading what I knew I had to

do, feeling the phantom pain of hurting a man I loved deeply.

"I really wish I could love Cole the way he wants," I admitted.

"I know, sweetie, I know. But don't worry, once he's gotten over you and he's recovered and back on the market, I'm calling dibs."

I stiffened. "What?"

"You heard me. But so you know, I didn't start checking out his tight ass until I could tell you were fallin' out of love with him. I'm not a vulture. I'm an opportunist is all. Gotta jump on chances when they come my way."

When I didn't comment, she asked in a reserved tone that revealed she was actually worried, "Should I not have said anything?"

I snorted. "About me having to break up with Cole, or you wanting to jump him?" I rubbed absently at my wrist, careful not to graze the red, inflamed puncture wounds on the back of my hand.

"Me bein' interested in him."

Birdie was too fierce to appear vulnerable, but like most everyone else, she had a soft side to her she rarely let others see.

"I wanted you to know," she added gently, "so it wasn't like I was sneaking around with my thoughts or anything. You're my best friend. You always come first for me. I never would want you to think I went behind your back to do anything. With Cole or anyone else."

I breathed in deeply, thinking, feeling, reflecting. Finally, I smiled at her back, though a bit sadly. "I'm glad you told me. And I'm equally glad Cole will end up with someone who'll love him right."

"I've been practicing a whole lot, so I'm sure I will."

I laughed, choosing to let judgment and rules and preconceived notions drift away. Life was too short for all that nonsense. Birdie was right. It was time to be true to myself—and do right by Cole in the best way I could now.

She laughed too, before asking, "So, tell me, which of the two sexy asses in your clinker do you like best? Or do you like both just as well? Mmm-mmmm, you know, no one says you have to choose between them..."

"That makes about as much sense as tits on a bull. No one can have two men at once."

"Maybe not just anyone can, but I've seen how they both look at you. You could."

I slapped her back again. She shrugged. "Just sayin'."

"Then you've done enough sayin' to last us. I'm a one-man kinda woman. One relationship is all the fuss I can handle."

"So you say…"

I hated it when she did that. "It's true, Bird. Why would I want two guys? I'm already in the process of letting down one really decent man."

"Okay, then which one do you like best?"

"Neither of 'em. I've got enough on my plate to keep me from thinkin' about them for, like, ever."

But then all I could do on the rest of the way to my office was think about both of them. And Cole.

By the time Jolene stopped in front of the jail, I was dizzy from all the fretting and the dragon poison and the two gigantic pains in my asses just inside.

I slid off Jolene with little grace and less stability, but I managed to do it on my own, asking Birdie to wait outside. "And tell Cole and my parents I'm good and that you're gonna stay to wait for me, will ya?"

I flicked a worried glance at them, drawing almost close enough that Cole would be able to see my eyes. If he did, he'd know something was wrong between us.

"Yeah, you got it, girl," Birdie said. "Now, hurry before they get here."

Hurrying wasn't in the cards for me that night, but I managed to stumble up the steps, lean heavily into the door, and pull it open. I made sure to look steady to my parents and Cole before I practically fell inside.

## CHAPTER 11
## Everything Burns with Devilish Grins

I only realized just how much the ride from Portal Platform to my office took out of me when I stumbled across the threshold. My thoughts still on Cole and my parents arriving outside, I struggled—but managed—to kick the door closed behind me. The instant it shut, my muscles finished turning to mush. *Mush.* It was as if not a bone remained in my entire body. Like Doc Holloway had sucked them right out through the dragon bite.

I figured it was the shock of a spectral dragon attack, the exhaustion of enduring all that pain, the weight of the increasingly complicated situation that s my duty to resolve, and the knowledge that I was going to have to break Cole's heart. It caught up to me all at once.

Suddenly, the hard, uncomfortable wooden floor of my office was looking mighty appealing. My eyelids grew heavy, the energy I'd had to converse with Birdie on the way over here spent. There was no reserve for me to dip into to hold myself up. My body had decided—all on its own—that it was going down.

What the hell. I'd let it. I surely didn't give a flying freaking freckle anymore.

My knees buckled; my arms weighed a hundred tons. Even my boobs felt unreasonably heavy. My head wobbled on my neck. My hand throbbed as if it had its very own beating heart.

I crumbled—but didn't smack into the floor.

Tiger was a blur of orange, white, and black—of animal elegance, grace, and magnificence.

From the other side of the office, he leapt—and when I dropped as if I'd stuffed my pockets with stones, my landing was soft and cushioned.

I sagged into him in relief, content to be with my best bud again, happy that he forgave me for throwing a mini hissy fit at him for getting a belly rub, as if I had a corner on that market. His belly was soft and fuzzy and perfect.

Leaning my head back, I straightened my legs from their current awkward angle and slumped all the way into him.

I sighed happily. This was great. I could sleep a whole week here—or at least until Tiger had to pee—just like this.

He purred deep in his chest, a rumble that vibrated beneath my head and back, soothing me. I settled more comfortably against him, bringing my pulsing arm to rest across my lap.

But he nudged me with his nose. I ignored him for the tug of sleep.

He prodded me again.

I dragged my eyelids up in slow motion as if they were as leaden as the rest of me. I stared into soft, concerned cat eyes.

"I'm good, T. Just gotta ... *zzzz*." It was the best I could do, and I wasn't entirely sure anyone other than Tiger could make out what spilled out of my mouth.

My eyes were on their way to closing again when I heard Letitia Lake, her voice shrill and grating. "Good gravy, Loretta. What the hell happened to you?"

Before I could properly register where she was talking to me from, her face was up in mine.

"You look plumb awful, girl." Her mouth and eyes attempted to settle into appropriate expressions of concern, but it didn't last long. She was already primping her already voluminous hair and looking between me and over her back repeatedly.

She was looking at Rhett or Zeke, or both of them, guaranteed. I didn't have to force my vision all that distance away to know it. If Letitia was anything, she was consistent in her priorities.

A moment later, Zeke appeared in front of me. His bright blue eyes blinked at me a few times before trailing across the length of my body. This time, I didn't feel the telltale heat of his attention; I was already feeling warm all over. Hot, in fact. Too hot. I suspected I had a fever.

"What happened?" Zeke asked, his voice an urgent insistence.

"Hmmmm," I said, wondering if they might be able to figure it out from that. Suddenly, I had no juice left at all.

"What's going on?" Rhett asked from within his cell—or at least, so I assumed. I couldn't see that far just then, my vision cloudy, but the jail had more magic than I did. No one could escape from the prison I placed them in without getting shocked half to death.

Tiger had been an additional—and possibly unnecessary—precaution. However, I didn't trust Rhett or Zeke one bit, so better safe than sorry, and that was before I knew Letitia was here with them when she shouldn't have been.

Raised voices filtered through the walls, but their words were muffled. My pulse whooshed through my head, making hearing difficult. The bite in my hand throbbed to the same rhythm, just half a second behind. I felt as if I were being pulled in two directions.

I tried to close my eyes. Sleep was far easier than all this.

But someone shook me. Hard.

*Mofo.* Didn't they know I was injured? I mumbled, *Go screw yourself, I'm gonna sleep now, thanks very much.* Or maybe that was just in my head?

Another brutal shake and I opened my eyes, if just to narrow them at … Zeke.

His handsome face was pulled into worried lines, the edges of his crystalline blue eyes crinkled. Their depths whirled hypnotically, seeming to draw me toward him.

Dammit. What was it with these gorgeous men who wouldn't leave me alone?

I closed my eyes and refused to open them even when the shaking grew more insistent. If they were gonna be stubborn as mules, I'd just have to be more persistent.

The tug of sleep became stronger until shouts sliced the elusive peace I kept reaching for. Then a door squealed. Damn that squeak. I was going to drown the hinges in grease ... just as soon as I could move.

More cries, running footsteps, a horse whinnying that sounded a lot like Jolene.

Wait, where was I again? I fluttered my eyelids open to look, but managed to make out nothing beyond blurred shapes and light before they closed again, this time of their own volition.

Tiger began chuffing in agitation beneath me, but I couldn't open my eyes. That would require strength I didn't have.

Besides, everything would feel better once I got a little sleep...

I was fond of gentle, leisurely awakenings, like when the sun filtered through my bedroom window in a warm, soothing embrace, lulling me back from the dream world. Indeed, one of my favorite things about Cole sleeping over was how introspective he was in the mornings—and cuddly.

I was not, however, fond of being shaken awake so brutally that my teeth smacked together, biting my tongue.

I snapped my eyes open exclusively to glare death rays at whomever dared mess with me like this.

Only it was my mom's face—not Zeke's as I expected—and her obvious panic swept away all my irritation.

I tried to sit up from where I was still slumped against Tiger, but she pressed my shoulders down.

"Why are you holding me down?" I asked. "What is it?"

My mom sighed in relief, her breath a hot breeze along my skin, smelling faintly of the spices she used in her signature lentil stew.

She sat back onto her haunches, looking at my dad over her shoulder, sighing once more. "Oh my beatin' heart. I can breathe again."

She was addressing my dad, but he wasn't the

only other one huddled around me. Birdie, Cole, Zeke, and Letitia were there too.

*And Rhett.*

"What in hell's bells is *he* doin' out of his cell?" I asked the group.

"I let him out," my dad said. "We need him."

I scoffed and tried to push up again. My mom lunged forward to press me back into Tiger's soft fur.

"Momma, lemme go already."

"No, honey. You ain't movin' till we know what's going on. You about scared the living daylights right out of me and your daddy."

Everyone, even Letitia, wore a similar expression: forehead crinkled, brows bunched together, mouth in a wavering, fidgety line.

But not Rhett. Not the motherfreaking thorn in my side.

When I looked at him, he grinned.

I snapped, "I put you in a cell! If you know what's good for you, you'll march your tight behind right back into it!"

His smile grew. His eyes twinkled. I wished I had the energy to kick him in the balls.

"But I have to save you, darlin'," he cooed.

"Don't you *darlin'* me. I don't need your saving."

Truth was, I felt about as spritely as a day-old carcass, buzzards flying around me, the flies buzzing. That still didn't mean I needed *him* to save me.

Though I was certain my face betrayed my thoughts, Rhett only crossed his arms in front of his chest, making his biceps bulge—and freaking winked at me.

"Oh, sweetheart, but I think you do need me to swoop in n' save you."

"Hey," Cole barked at him, moving to block his view of me. "She's not your sweetheart. She's *mine*. You'd better mind your manners or I'll knock you so hard you'll see tomorrow today."

"That sounds like fun. I've always wanted to look into the future." Rhett's eyes gleamed some more, and Cole stepped into his personal space.

Zeke knelt next to me, rolling his eyes. It was my dad who moved between Cole and Rhett, a hand on either of their chests.

"Cool it, boys. There'll be plenty of time for ass kickin' later. Remember Loretta."

"She's all I'm thinkin' about," Cole said, and I sighed loudly before remembering to hold back. It wasn't Cole's fault I was already anticipating having to cut things off with him.

My thoughts were sluggish, my skin too warm. My pulse was too noticeable.

*The bite. The dragon. And the note.*

All at once, I remembered everything that had happened and glanced down at my hand.

"Oh shit."

Everyone turned their attention to the festering puncture wounds, a whole row of them spanning the width of my hand.

"That doesn't look good," I mumbled.

The small holes in my flesh were a bright fiery orange that glowed as if they contained roiling lava in their depths. The flesh around them appeared sunburned, all the way up to the tourniquet squeezing down on my forearm. It was as red as when Lonnie Marr stayed out in the blazing sun all day and forgot his hat. His face had peeled for two weeks straight.

I bit my lip. "So, what? I passed out from the bite?"

My mom squeezed my other hand. "Just for a hot second, honey. No one'll hold it against you. And if they're stupid enough to think you're weak after gettin' bit by a *dragon*, then I'll kick them right in the rump till they remember to think better on it."

Jolene whinnied outside again. I singled out Birdie. "Will you go tell 'er that I'm fine?"

My best friend, who was usually all smiles and a bouncy step, shook her head at me. "I'm not gonna lie to Jo."

"What's that mean?"

"That means we don't know if you're fine, woman. Just look at you! You got holes in your hand worse than those nasty-ass pimples Ashlyn used to get that were so bad we wouldn't even eat her doughnuts, and you know that's bad as bad gets. Her doughnuts are plumb *amazin'*. You're scratched up all over, got rips in your shirt, like ya got dragged by a stampeding herd of stallions. And worse..."

"Worse? What could be worse?" I asked. "You're already making me sound like I got Declan James beat, and he sets fire to shit without meaning to. He's constantly got burnt black patches on his clothes."

Birdie didn't answer me right away, and *that* made me worry more than anything. Birdie wasn't known for using the skill of forethought or for minding her tongue. She ran a hand nervously through her hair, something I wasn't sure I'd ever seen her do.

My gut clenched and my pulse accelerated, the throbbing distracting. Tiger whined beneath me, something he also rarely did.

"What is it? Tell me already," I growled, all the while thinking maybe I didn't actually want to know.

Everyone hemmed and hawed like the bloody cat got their tongue.

"Y'all shouldn't tiptoe around her," Rhett finally said. "She's a grown woman."

As if to prove his point, he dragged his gaze leisurely across my body.

I frowned at him and barked, "What the hell's goin' on, y'all? You'd better tell me right this second!"

I expected Rhett to tell me, but it was Zeke who cleared his throat and said, "You're glowing."

"This ain't the time for funnies, Zeke. Tell me what's really goin' on and *now*."

A sheen of tears glistened in my mom's eyes, and my dad's lower lip trembled before he ran a hand across his mouth to cover it up. Birdie looked ready to jump out of her skin, and Cole kept smoothing his hands across his face.

"I'm *not* glowing," I insisted, removing my uninjured hand from my mom's clutches to wave it around in front of me. "See? Normal skin. No glow. Same as always."

"Well, it's your eyes that are glowing ... for one," Zeke said. "And—"

"And your boobs," Rhett interjected.

Zeke's lips pursed after a scoff slipped out. "It's not her boobs."

Cole sidestepped my dad to get up in Rhett's face again. "Stop lookin' at her boobs. They're not for you to look at!"

Coolly, Rhett smiled at Cole, reminding me of a coyote about to nab a rabbit. "I can look at whatever I want to, and her breasts are mighty beautiful."

Cole shoved forward, but my dad pushed a hand against his chest. Cole grunted in heated frustration. "Levi, let me at 'im already. He can't keep sayin' the shit he says about Loretta."

"No, he can't," my dad said. "But now's not the time, son. Loretta needs us first."

"Loretta doesn't need any of you," Rhett said, the arrogant ass that he was. "She needs *me*."

Cole sidestepped my dad again. "Like hell she does." He pulled his fist back, ready to let it fly.

"You will both quit goin' round your asses to get to your elbows," my dad said, pulling up to his full height, his bear simmering close to the surface, ready to break loose. "Focus. Or I'll make you—both of you."

Rhett tsked, and I thought my daddy might kill him then and there and spare me a whole load of trouble. Proving he was as stupid as I thought, Rhett ignored my dad's growing rage, even as it sizzled in the air, instead tossing his head to clear the strand of hair that had slipped into an eye, as if the idjit didn't have a care in the world. Then he casually said, "You should be thanking me for my help. It's not every day I offer it."

That was when I braved the swirling vertigo and thumping in my head to tilt my chin down. My boobs were indeed *not* glowing, though I noticed that my shirt was torn across them, my bra largely exposed. But that wasn't what held my attention. Oh no, revealing tears didn't come close to being important when I saw that the area above my breastbone *was* glowing.

Glowing.

Motherfreaking flapping *glowing*.

The light wasn't particularly bright. It didn't put off enough luminosity to draw my eye before I looked at it directly.

Now, though, I couldn't look away. My mouth

hung open, my eyes bugged out, and I felt like my skin would soon peel off all over my body from the heat running beneath it.

Approximately the same size and shape as the dragon's egg, the area glowed the color of the quasi lava inside the puncture wounds.

I swallowed ... and then touched the spot. Other than feeling warm, it seemed no different than the rest of me.

"Are my eyes..." I paused and tried again. "My eyes, are they doin' the same thing? They're really hot."

"Yes," Zeke answered right away. "You have dragon magic inside you."

My throat went dry in an instant, my question a mere whisper. "What'd you just say?"

"You have dragon magic building inside you."

"Dragon magic? Seriously?"

He nodded solemnly. One glance at everyone else confirmed he wasn't pulling my leg.

Assuming I believed him, I couldn't decide whether to be glad or terrified. I'd always wanted magic—of any sort.

"That's why you need me," Rhett said, stalking away from both the posturing black bear shifter that was my dad, and Cole, the mage who was now sparking blue magic in his open palms.

*Dragon magic, dragon magic, dragon magic,* was on a continual loop through my mind, and yet I forced out: "And why would I need you? Surely it's not because of your charmin' personality." I even managed a rough, disparaging chuckle.

"You'll come for what I am. You'll stay because of who I am."

"That makes no damn sense. What the hell do you even mean?"

A devilish grin was my only immediate response. It told me the man had far too many secrets...

CHAPTER 12

*Not Even Dragons Poop Gold Nuggets*

Just when I'd discovered the strength to press Rhett for answers instead of all that hogwash he was spewing, the door to my office flew open so hard that plaster splintered when it knocked against the wall.

I shifted against Tiger to direct my newfound strength at the brute who'd entered my office like a dust storm, but hesitated when I found Coby Rae standing there.

The woman made no secret about having a crush on me. She was worse than Rhett in the way she blatantly checked me out.

Usually.

Now her eyeballs were vibrating in their sockets, and the normally brazen woman appeared unsure.

"Loretta?" she said, softer than she might have ever spoken before. "What ... what's goin' on here? Jolene and Triple C are goin' crazy out there, and they're settin' off all the other horses."

Triple C was short for Chocolate Chip Cookie, Birdie's Appaloosa gelding, so named for the multitude of brown spots peppered across his coat.

"Why ... why do ya look like a lamppost, all juiced up with Tucker's magic?" she went on without waiting for a response from any of us. "And why are you wearin' Doc's belt around your arm?"

"How'd you know it was Doc's belt?" Birdie asked, as if that were the most important point to unpack from the scene.

Coby Rae pointed in my general direction. "I recognize the buckle. She's the only one with a unicorn on hers."

I didn't even bother glancing down to confirm. I had my priorities straight—or at least straighter. A new wave of heat surged inside my body, hurrying me along. I had no idea what was about to happen to me.

"You didn't come in here just because of the horses," I told Coby Rae, who was never one to concern herself much with others' business—unless it pertained to my curves.

"I didn't..."

"And?" I pressed. "So what is it?"

"Well, I heard you got bit by a dragon." That was a given. News spread through Traitor's Den faster than an unchecked wildfire. "But seein' you like this, all"—she waved both hands in my general direction—"you know..."

I *didn't* know, actually. But I wasn't inclined to ask for details. The way everyone kept looking at me as if I were about to keel over, or perhaps catch fire, was sufficient to paint a picture.

"Go on," I said. "You obviously tore in here like a rabid 'coon's on your heels for a reason."

"Yeah, don't worry 'bout that. It's nothin'."

At this point, I was pretty sure I'd croak from impatience before I died from any other ailment. "Tell me or go, but whatever you do, best be doin' it now." I didn't bother saying I had pressing matters to attend to; Coby Rae wasn't stupid.

"Fine," she said. "It's Kiki."

Birdie drew in a gasp that hissed like a whistle. "What's wrong with Kiki?"

"Coby Rae didn't say nothin' about something being wrong with her, Birdie," I admonished, though my stomach was busy sinking, proving me a hypocrite.

Kiki had come through the pocket portal around five years before, quickly winning over the hearts of Denners with her easygoing, lovable nature. Even Declan James loved her, and he was a sourpuss.

"Well, is somethin' wrong with you?" Coby Rae asked me. "'Cause if there is, then there's something wrong with Kiki too."

"Then spit it out already," I said, working very hard not to snap at her.

My heart already hammering in my throat, Saxon Silver came barreling through the door, yelling, "Loretta, come quick like. Kiki's—"

Then he saw me and faltered. "Damn. Well, Kiki's in better shape then you are, I reckon."

I rolled my head on my neck while holding in a mega load of frustration, then forced a smile. From how everyone cringed, I was guessing it revealed how unstable I felt. "What in the dickens is goin' on with Kiki? Someone spit it out in under two seconds or I'm gonna—"

"Wait, two seconds from when you finish talkin'," Coby Rae asked. "Or from when you said it?"

My scary smile deepened. She took a step back though she wasn't near me.

"Take your pick," I said dangerously. It was

entirely possible I was about to blow up into a ball of raging fire. If I did, I was thinking maybe I should take all of them with me, put an end to the suspense once and for all.

Saxon, clearly unintimidated by me in my current volatile state, walked closer. "Kiki's glowin', but not like you. Not like she's about to explode like a whole bushel o' dynamite. She's flickerin', comin' in and out. Reminds me of the pocket portal when it flares to life."

"Is she in pain?" I asked urgently. There was no gentler creature than Kiki, and none less deserving of suffering.

"Don't think so. She looks happy. Like she does after she's been cuddlin' all day."

"Good." I pushed up, brushing away my mom when she attempted to keep me in place once more. "Help me to her."

Once my mom saw I was getting up no matter what she thought, she angled herself under my good arm, wrapping it around her shoulders. She heaved upward, and Tiger slowly rose to his feet, lifting me along with him.

Even standing with support, I could tell there was no way I should do so on my own. Cole, reading my cues, went to wrap an arm around my waist, mindful not to touch my injury—but Rhett grunted. Loudly.

Then he growled.

He stalked over to me, his eyes glowing as brightly as I imagined mine were.

He muscled Cole out of the way without a word and scooped me off my feet, causing my mom to let go with a squeal.

"She's not going anywhere," he said.

I didn't say a thing, too stunned to speak for a moment.

"It's too dangerous. Y'all don't understand what's happening to her," he insisted.

Finally, I snapped out of my shock at being manhandled like I was a delicate damsel in distress. "Put. Me. Down."

"You heard the woman," Cole said from somewhere behind us, and I could picture his face, growing red with anger.

"I heard her, but she doesn't know what's best for her," said the dumbass holding me.

"Excuse me?" I asked in the kind of slow, menacing tone that had my mom and dad flexing to come to my aid, and Coby Rae looking ready to bolt like a skittish pony, when I'd never pegged her for being squeamish of a little tussle.

"I'm willin' to pretend you didn't just say what it sounds like you said," I started, "so long as you put me down right this second." In truth, I'd *never* forget what he said, and I'd never let *him* forget it either. But he didn't have to know that just yet.

"No," said the village idjit.

Zeke popped up in my view. "Rhett, stop being a dick."

"I'm not being a dick. She shouldn't move or the dragon magic might react to her even more."

I froze in his hold. "React how?"

He looked down at me. For once, his constant arrogance was absent.

"I don't know."

"Well, then—"

"No," he interrupted me. "You didn't let me finish. I might not know exactly what will happen in your specific case, but I do know, *very* well, how unstable dragon magic is. Trust me, you don't want to be taking any additional risks right now."

"Trust *you*? Why would I trust *you*? You're cagey and brash and—"

"And disrespectful," Cole inserted.

"That too," I said, wishing Cole hadn't interrupted my flow. I was just getting started with the litany of adjectives I had set aside for Rhett.

Zeke placed a cool hand on my shoulder, making me realize just how hot my flesh was. "I'm the first to tell you not to trust him. He's a scoundrel, a womanizer, a thief, a—"

"You're not helping, Zeke," Rhett ground out.

Zeke cleared his throat and stared me in the eyes. "He's your best chance to survive this."

"Wait," my mom piped up, "are you sayin' there's a chance my baby girl won't ... survive ... this?" Her voice caught.

Zeke looked at me while he answered: "I'm saying ... Rhett has his many, *many* issues. He's obnoxious, quick to anger, acts without caring about the consequences, and I feel like punching him in the gonads half the time. But..."

He trailed the back of his hand along one of my cheeks in the gentlest of touches. I leaned into it, aching for the coolness of it, but too fast it was gone, back at his side.

"But Rhett's literally the only one who can help her now."

My mom whimpered softly and my dad wrapped her in his arms, pulling her against his broad chest.

"And why's that?" I asked in a croak.

Rhett pulled me more tightly against his chest. "Because I'm a dragon shifter."

A shocked inhale sliced through the silence, and I was surprised to discover it came from Saxon. I'd never witnessed the dwarf shocked by anything, and he lived in Traitor's Den, where weird was a way of life.

"A dragon shifter?" Saxon asked, the question sounding sacred from his reverence.

"I am," Rhett said.

Zeke palmed Rhett on the back, making me jump in his arms. "And not just any dragon shifter."

"Enough," Rhett growled, and I growled too. It was like pulling teeth with this man just to get some basic information! "They know what they need to know to trust me."

"Um, I still don't trust you," I said.

Birdie chuckled, cutting through some of the tension in the room. "That's my girl."

Rhett scowled down at me. "You don't need to trust me. But you do need to let me help you."

"And if I don't?"

"Then you'll probably die. The dragon fire'll eat you up from the inside out. All that'll remain will be a charred husk."

Given what I was currently experiencing, his prediction was entirely believable. My insides were too hot. Too overwhelming.

With a wink, Rhett added, "And it'd be a shame to let a body as fine as yours burn to a crisp."

"A charmer, this one," Birdie said, and I could hear the smirk in her words.

"How do I know you're tellin' the truth?" I asked Rhett, looking to Zeke too. "All you've done since you got here is cause trouble."

"Loretta," Saxon interjected, "he's a dragon shifter. You shouldn't talk to him like that."

I snorted. "I don't care if he shits gold nuggets. I'll talk to him how I damn well please, and how he's earned."

"Spicy," Rhett said. "I like it."

"I'm not after you likin' me." But then I couldn't help a quick glance at Cole, who looked ready to punch someone, preferably the man holding me in his arms, but anyone might do at this point.

"Then we're even," Rhett said. "I don't need you to like me either. But I do want to save you."

"Why?"

"'Cause I think I might like you despite your best intentions otherwise. And because no one's ever locked me up before."

I felt my eyebrow quirk. "And you ... liked that?"

"I loved it. I like challenges."

"Watch your mouth," Cole snapped.

Without swiveling anything but his head, Rhett faced my boyfriend. "Make me."

Cole lunged at Rhett. My dad grabbed his shoulder to hold him back, and Saxon wrapped both arms around his thigh. Birdie smiled like this was great entertainment, and Coby Rae ducked her head outside.

All of that dislodged a sudden thought. "If it's true that you're a dragon shifter—"

"It's true," Zeke said. "I wish it weren't, but it is."

"Then you might be able to read the note the dragon left. Or maybe it wasn't the dragon, I dunno, but it was in the bottle."

"What note?" Zeke asked urgently.

I let my mom explain about the runes none of us recognized while I attempted to dig into the pocket of my jean shorts to retrieve the message, not an easy feat when I ached all over, my head was fuzzy, and I was folded into Rhett's strong arms. But just as I almost had it out, a scream tore through the night.

My first thought was, *Damn, will this day* ever *end?* Luckily, what I said aloud was, "Let's go."

When Rhett hesitated, I added, "*Now*. I'm the sheriff and this is my town." Never mind that I wasn't particularly thrilled to claim ownership of it.

Rhett didn't move so much as an inch as Coby Rae, Birdie, and even Cole rushed outside to see what was happening. But then he was running, charging out the door of the sheriff's office like he was a bull who'd caught sight of a taunting red flag, clutching me close to his chest, taking care not to jostle me.

Zeke, Saxon, and my parents were a step behind us, and Tiger shadowed Rhett's every step as if my good friend trusted him about as much as I did.

*Not a bit.*

CHAPTER 13

*Hear Tiger Roar*

Rhett's pounding steps shook the wooden stairs as he tore down them.

Since my horse was tied up right outside, I would have liked to reassure her so she wouldn't keep whinnying and worrying. But any hopes at shouting a passing "I'm fine"—likely a lie—were dashed as we emerged into chaos.

Denners crowded the wide street, obscuring the source of the commotion, that heart-stopping scream that still had my adrenaline pumping—or maybe that was also the dragon magic. No one had told me yet exactly what having it coursing through me meant, only that it wasn't good.

People and creatures searched for the problem with tangible desperation, jerking their heads in every direction, asking anyone looking their way what was going on. Knowing Denners, they could have been motivated to be the first to learn the news as much as to help. There was a little of everything in Traitor's Den.

Tiger drew to a stop next to Rhett and me, surveying the pandemonium with us. People jetted to and fro like wayward ducklings, whipping toward any loud sound. Horses neighed and stomped, tied off to either side of the thoroughfare.

Had I been my usual self, I would've called them to attention. I had a good set of lungs on me.

If that didn't work, I would've enlisted Big Bertha to do the job. Given that I could barely move, I glanced over at Tiger instead.

Though Rhett was tall, my furry friend was massive. His head nearly reached the dragon shifter's shoulder. "Help me out?" I asked him.

Tiger nodded and I told Rhett, "You're gonna wanna move away from Tiger for a hot sec."

A brow raised in perfect roguish fashion, he said, "Hot sex, what?"

I slapped him with my usable hand, but the effort was pathetic. My arm flopped weakly back against my legs. "I mean it. *Move*. Now."

I expected him to resist or to ask questions, but

to my surprise he jogged away from Tiger, sliding to a stop only when he about ran smack dab into Brewster, the unfriendly neighborhood pygmy troll.

Brewster, in his usual alarming attire of chaps that revealed a full view of round little bare butt cheeks, tipped his cowboy hat back so he could glare up at Rhett, revealing a sliver of the shockingly violet fro-hawk underneath. His mouth opened, but before he could say a word, Tiger roared.

And when Tiger roared, the only option was to stop whatever you were doing to give him your full attention.

Despite the fact that Tiger had been stuck in his animal form for over a decade, he often acted much like a human, save for the fact that he couldn't talk. He was highly intelligent and understood everything happening around him; he was even sophisticated enough not to lick his undercarriage when I was paying attention.

But when he let loose, Tiger was all big cat and terrifying predator. Large, sharp teeth and an enormous maw. Every instinct I had told me my life would soon come to a swift, painful end, and I'd be inside his belly. His bellow rattled teeth and windowpanes, and made the horses jumpy even though Tiger had never nipped at a single one of them.

His roar went on longer than necessary. He didn't get to do this often, and I couldn't blame him for not wanting to hold back. He was a major *badass* often presumed to have the demeanor of a fluffball kitty cat.

By the time Tiger finally brought his call to a close, everyone around him stood visibly shaken, hair windswept from the power of his magic.

"We can go back to him now," I whispered to Rhett, unwilling to distract from the loud silence that had overcome the street. No one moved. Everyone stared at Tiger. Magnolia Roone, the mayor's wife, discreetly wiped away a fine trail of drool from where her mouth had hung open. Letitia Lake's already fluffed hair looked like a meringue about to roll off her head.

Surprising me again, Rhett quietly walked back to Tiger's side, where I offered my empowered friend the kind of maniacal grin he deserved.

Then I yelled, "Now, who the dickens screamed and why?" Only, my words came out as garbled as the rest of me felt, and at half the volume I intended. After the force of Tiger's call-to-attention, they fell flat.

Zeke drew up to stand beside us while my dad moved next to Tiger, announcing, "My daughter's been through a lot today already, protectin' this town. Don't make her repeat herself."

Levi Ray brought a hand to rest on either hip, just above his holsters, and tipped his head down to stare up at everyone from under the brim of his hat. It was his signature move, and it'd been working on me for as long as I could remember.

It also worked on other Denners, apparently.

Hank Henry stepped into the middle of the crowd, sweeping off his hat to hold it in front of him. Everyone else stepped back, giving him ample room.

Alone now in an open circle, Hank Henry hesitated.

"Well?" I pressed, working very hard to inject authority into everything I said. My scalp was so hot I could barely focus.

Hank Henry cleared his throat.

"Hank Henry, it ain't the time for hemming and hawing. Spit it out already." *Before I pass out again right here in front of all y'all.*

"Well ... it was me that done called for everybody to, ah, assemble."

"You mean, screamed like a—" Birdie was saying when Cole elbowed her.

See? Cole was such a good guy. Birdie was, well, Birdie. She'd never been interested in learning when it was appropriate to speak her mind, or, more importantly, when it wasn't.

"Why'd you call for us?" I asked Hank Henry, glad that my voice didn't crack from strain this time. "Is it Kiki?"

At the mention of Kiki, the crowd interrupted their stunned quiet to whisper at each other.

"What's goin' on with Kiki?" someone asked, while another more frantic voice said, "She's alright, ain't she?"

Panic was swiftly building all over again.

"Don't make me ask Tiger to roar at y'all another time," I said. "You know I will."

No one said another word, not even Hank Henry.

"Oh, for crikey's sake," I muttered, wishing I could hop out of Rhett's arms to go slap some sense into the man. "Hank Henry, don't just stand there like the porch light's on but no one's home. What happened already?"

He nodded like he was finally letting good sense in, exposing the thinning top of his hair.

"Right. So Kiki's flashin' and changin' and all sorts of weird stuff."

I waited for more. In Traitor's Den, *weird* was just the way things were.

"She's glowin' ... kinda like you, but not."

With effort, I swallowed a groan. "Can anyone help Hank Henry here get to the end of what he's tryin' to say before he's passed by a herd a turtles? Where is Kiki?"

Henrietta Hammer moved next to Hank Henry, saying, "Kiki's right inside Sharmayne's place. And she looks like she's feelin' just fine, happy and all. She's just real different lookin', like she's got a mega dose of magic we had no earthly idea about."

"Excellent." *I hoped.* "Thank you, Henrietta ... and Hank Henry." Then, to my temporary steed, "Take me to see her, Rhett."

The crowd parted for us like we were a wave about to crash onto shore. I couldn't help but wonder how much of that was out of respect for me and my office, along with concern for Kiki, and how much was due to the fact that I probably looked scarier than whatever was going on with the magical creature. I sure felt like everyone *should* be giving me a wide berth. *I* didn't even want to deal with whatever mess was cooking inside me.

With Tiger leading the way, and Zeke, my parents, Birdie, and Cole keeping pace, we entered the saloon, empty except for the glorious koala sitting in the middle of it, like a petite, furry queen.

Kiki had always possessed an innate radiance that touched everyone around her. Her joy was contagious, and it was the main reason why she never had enough time to snuggle with everyone who wanted to. She was every Denner's favorite, even of the most sour-tempered among us—a four-way tie between Brewster the pygmy troll; Saxon the dwarf; Declan James, official curmudgeon of Traitor's Den; and Lily White, the cantankerous old witch who hadn't been much mourned after she died.

But where Kiki had been a lovely, sweet koala before, she was a glorious magical creature now. Her fur was no longer a flat gray, but now an iridescent violet that shimmered beneath the dim lights of the saloon. A soft, silvery white patch crested her chest and capped her paws. But it was her ears that had changed the most. No longer the small round nubs they'd been, they'd grown and morphed into silver-hewn shapes that mimicked tree branches. And at their points? Delicate white flowers rimmed in bright pink.

Her tail had grown longer too, bushier, with a silver dusting across its fur. But it was her eyes that captivated me most. Like my eyes, they glowed. Unlike mine, I wanted to dive into their depths and never emerge.

Small bright moons, they beamed compassion, love, and *magic*.

Everyone else who entered the saloon after us slowed reverently, removing their hats as if we were in the presence of a god. I suspected Kiki was as close to one as we would ever get in Traitor's Den, a town so wholly removed from the rest of the world.

"Wow," I finally whispered, when nothing else seemed to do her transformation justice.

Rhett asked, "She hasn't always been this way? Able to transform into this form?"

"No." I smiled, forgetting the torturous burn inside me more easily than before. "She's always been magnificent in her own way, but never like this. She only ever looked like a regular koala, though she was always special, and not just 'cause she's the only koala in town."

"When did she change like this?" he asked everyone.

Emmaline Bay, confectioner extraordinaire, shrugged. "No longer than a while ago. In the last hour or two."

Emmaline didn't care much for exactitude in anything but her candy making. Luckily for her, her candy was delicious enough to make up for her shortcomings.

"Was it when the dragon magic hit Loretta?" Rhett asked.

"And Bobbie Sue!"

I recognized Ashton Blu's voice, though he was somewhere behind me. He'd finally remembered his loyalty to his friend.

"Seems about right," Emmaline said, and immediately after we all waited for someone with a better sense of time to confirm.

"That's on the money," Sharmayne piped up from behind the bar, rounding it toward us while tying on her apron. "Y'all charged off to Pocket Portal makin' an awful racket, then around when I figure you'da had just enough time to make it there, Kiki started whining. I worried, 'course, and raced upstairs to see what she was goin' on about. But by the time I got there she was her happy self again. She followed me downstairs, then next time I checked on 'er, she looked like this."

As one, we all studied Kiki again. A placid, beaming smile spread across her face.

"Wow," I mumbled under my breath another time. "She really is magnificent."

"She sure as shit is," Sharmayne said.

"Think it was the dragon magic?" Zeke asked.

Only after a beat did I realize that he was talking only to Rhett.

The dragon shifter pressed his lips together in a tight line, making the scruff along his face seem darker, and finally nodded. "Yeah, that has to be what happened. I felt the power of it too."

"Wait, *what*?" I asked. "You *felt* the magic from all the way over at Portal Platform? Inside the jail?"

He looked down at me, and for a moment I felt as if I could lose myself to the depths of his eyes as easily as I could Kiki's. Cole must've noticed too, because he scowled and moved to position himself as close to me as possible while I remained in another man's arms. Soon, he'd begin arguing that he should carry me instead.

I hurried on, ready to be unhanded entirely.

"You're *sure* the dragon magic did this to Kiki?" I asked Rhett, insisting on total clarity.

"It had to've."

Zeke added, "Dragon magic is volatile, unpredictable, and strong as it gets. I've never heard of it doing anything like this to a creature that wasn't already connected to the dragon magic, but I'd bet it could do it. I've seen it do crazy, miraculous things."

"Are you a ... you know ... too?" I asked, unsure whether I wanted everyone to know what Rhett was yet, though the rumor mill would make sure everyone did before long.

Zeke snorted like my suggestion was an affront. "No, I am not."

I smiled tightly. It looked like I was going to have to twist his arm for more information later. Once I could properly use both of mine.

"So what's it, ah, gonna do to me?" I asked softly, well aware that everyone was hanging on my every word.

When neither Rhett nor Zeke answered right away, my mom sucked in a loud breath, waiting, anticipating, fretting as only a mother could.

"Well, dammit? Give it to me already."

I registered the setup I gave Rhett only after I spoke, but he didn't take the bait for yet another of his suggestive innuendos.

Which could only mean one thing.

Whatever answer he had to my question wasn't that I'd turn into a gloriously happy magical creature like Kiki.

"If you're not gonna answer me, then put me down—"

"I don't know exactly what'll happen to you," Rhett said. "I've seen it do both magnificent and terrible things."

I swallowed around a throat that had thickened with a sudden swell of emotion, nodding. With so many eyes on me, I wasn't about to reveal how freaked out his comment made me.

"The good news is," Zeke said, "that dragon magic works fast. We'll know soon."

"How soon?" my dad asked, my mom clutching his arm.

"*Soon* soon."

Oh joy, Zeke was being about as exact as Emmaline.

"But first," Rhett said, and I wanted to shrink away from the tension in his voice, "things are gonna get a lot worse before they get better. If—" He stopped mid-sentence, revealing he wasn't all brute.

I completed his obvious thought, however. "*If* they get better. Meaning, they might not."

Rhett and Zeke nodded solemnly.

"That's right," Zeke said. "There are no guarantees when it comes to this kind of magic."

Rhett's gaze trailed across my bare legs and stomach to rest on the swells of my breasts. "Such a shame to maybe waste a body like this one."

Annnnd he was back to being the brute I knew him to be.

I growled, "Put me down so I can land one on you where it counts."

"No."

"No?" My tone was dangerous, but Tiger's growl and my dad's threatening grunt were more so.

"Fine," Rhett said, lowering me slowly. "But don't say I didn't warn you."

"You didn't warn me about a single concrete thing, you ass—"

I sagged, leaning all my weight into Rhett while Tiger rushed around so he'd be behind me in case I fell again—a real possibility.

"Oh," I uttered, as the burning fire transformed into unbearable full-body tingles that overpowered my every thought.

Then like a prissy maiden—which I was most certainly *not*—I fainted.

CHAPTER 14

*I'm Okay Really I Am,
AKA Wishful
Thinking*

"Wait, I didn't faint, y'all," I mumbled, aware that I likely sounded drunker than Buster Brane after a long evening of grieving his wife's adulterous tendencies.

My tongue felt thicker than a felled tree trunk and just as unwieldy. "I didn't, I swear."

But I hadn't yet been able to open my eyes, so I wasn't sure who was buying the bullshit I was selling.

"I'mokayreallyIam," I slurred as the sounds of my surroundings reached me again all of a sudden as if I'd jacked up the volume.

It sounded like every Denner who could cram themselves into Sharmayne's saloon was talking all at once. I couldn't pick out a single thread of conversation beyond a few panicked mentions of my name.

Tingles continued to mingle with unbearable heat within every part of my body as I used my uninjured hand to manually push up one of my eyelids—and stare straight up at the heads of far too many people. My mom's face was nearest, staring at me with her wide, doe eyes that glistened in the low, red lighting of the place. Sharmayne might've rejected the whorehouse functionality built into her establishment, but she kept some major elements of the décor, claiming it was easier this way instead of owning up to her sometimes tawdry tastes.

"I'mkayMomma," I said, moving my hand from my eyelid to discover I could keep one open myself.

"I'll be dipped in shit and rolled in cracker crumbs," my momma said, her words reaching me only vaguely garbled. "You are most surely *not* okay, Loretta Maybelle. We're takin' you home right this second, and don't you try to argue with me 'bout it."

"Un-unh." I started shaking my head but soon realized that only intensified the cottony thumping. Holding it perfectly still, I willed my second eye open instead and finally noticed I was back in Rhett's muscular arms. Tiger stood directly beside me, growling regularly in agitation.

"I'mmmfine." My eyes might've rolled back into my head a bit, so I repeated myself for good measure.

My mom's hands came to her hips and her eyes narrowed.

*Uh-oh.*

"You got yourself a head full a stump water if you think I'm gonna let you keep pushin' yerself till there ain't nothin' left to push. You give enough of yourself to this town. You can't give more than you have to give."

She tilted her chin up in resolve; it was a move I didn't see often from her. "We're takin' you home, end of story."

Birdie and Cole were on either side of my mom, looking from her to me and back again. Neither one of them was going to interfere and take my side on this one, I knew it. They weren't cowards in most things, but no one in their right minds messed with a protective momma of any sort.

Once my mom made up her mind about something, no one was gonna change it. So I tried a different tactic.

"Don't think I can make the trip."

"You won't be walkin', honey. We'll let this strong young man take you home. He won't mind."

Rhett grunted but said nothing. Cole frowned but didn't correct her.

"Everything's swirly, Momma," I said, grateful to

find my thoughts clearer again. "I wanna be set down right here." I pointed limply at the nearest table. "I just need a few minutes. I feel like I was rode hard and put away wet, that's all."

"Did that dragon bite you so hard that you got to thinkin' I was born yesterday? *That is not all*. You heard what Rhett said. You shouldn't move or it might get worse, and it's already bad as bad gets from the looks of ya."

"Exactly why I should be put down right here. Less movin', less jostlin', better all around."

After enough back and forth to make me half wish I *had* fainted so I wouldn't have to deal with my mother in momma-bear mode, Rhett finally helped me into a chair at a neighboring table.

Immediately, Tiger stationed himself around my seat so no one could get to me without going through him first. I tried to offer him a grateful smile, but knew I failed when he whined louder than before.

If some crazy magic were inside him, hurting him, I'd be out of my mind with concern too.

I'd give him extra belly rubs later—once I could think straight again.

My mom pulled out the chair across from me,

claiming it; Tiger's large body blocked off the other two.

I struggled to keep track of the most pressing matters. A dragon egg, dragon magic, dragon shifter, and a note. Plus Kiki and Bobbie Sue.

I had to get my shit together and keep it that way.

"Shar," I called out as loudly as I could manage to be heard over the chaotic din.

The bar matron bustled over to my side, opting to give Tiger a wide berth instead of the usual petting. The woman had always been able to read a room.

She fiddled with the lace on her apron, searching my eyes while she did so. "What can I do for ya, honey? You're lookin' a little rough round the edges."

"You got anything stronger than a Sirens on the Rocks?"

Her thin eyebrows arched. "Not at the moment. But you know me, I do love a good challenge. I'll whip somethin' new up, just for you. What do ya need?"

"Somethin' strong enough to overcome the dragon magic burnin' inside me and makin' it tough to think straight. I got work to do"—I held up a hand to halt my mom's protests—"and I aim to do it."

"You need rest, Loretta Maybelle," my mom said.

"I'll rest when I'm dead." Then to Sharmayne, "Do your magic for me, Shar."

She nodded and tapped the table. "I got an idea tidying up already." Then she hustled away.

While I waited, I sank into my chair and kicked my feet up on to one of the empties. Now that I was out of Rhett's arms, I began to unwind; there was no way I could relax while he was holding me.

Searching the bar, I caught sight of all the expected faces. Many Denners still watched me, but others had already claimed tables of their own and were ordering drinks. Ellie Mae Sanders, one of a few waitresses who helped Sharmayne out, was taking their requests.

That's when the milling crowd parted to make way for Kiki, who continued to beam like a soft moon. I could stare at her all night long, I thought while she ambled toward us, her face placid. She was a little furry goddess among mortals.

She dawdled on four legs, unhurried, until she reached me, then climbed up onto my lap without so much as a single concerned glance at the giant man-eater hovering protectively over me.

Tiger ceased his growling at her arrival, and soon she curled up on my lap, closed her eyes, and appeared to go to sleep.

I blinked at her, unable to resist a smile. If Kiki didn't think there was anything to worry about, then maybe I shouldn't either.

Then again, Kiki was so Zen she could probably take a nap during the apocalypse, trusting that everything would be fine in the end on a big-picture level.

Sharmayne sidled up, sliding a drink in front of me. "Ain't she just as cute as a bug's ear?"

That Kiki was. Her now-violet fur shimmered with silver highlights, and the soft branches that crowned her head pointed off my lap, the delicate flowers adorning them a fragrant bouquet.

Kiki was beyond cute. She was otherworldly.

I reached for the reddish-orange, fizzing and bubbling drink Sharmayne had brought. It was in a clear glass that was hot to the touch. I wanted to tell her that the last thing I needed was more heat, but even half out of my mind I knew better than to question the woman who kept me liquored up on the regular.

I adjusted my injured hand so it lay across Kiki's back; her body rose and fell with steady, deep breaths. With the other, I took my first sip, feeling Sharmayne's attention on me like a sunbeam.

When the drink first hit my mouth, it was an explosion of cherry and orange flavors that stung and tickled my tongue. Then everything burned as it went down, all the way into the pit of my stomach.

Just as I began to fear that Sharmayne might have let me down for the first time ever, and that I'd start sweating again soon, my entire body cooled. As if I'd imbibed a gust of frigid air instead of moonshine, I started feeling more like my usual self.

I beamed up at her. "Well, ain't that just the berries. Shar, you did it. That cleared me right up."

Sharmayne smiled so wide that her one crooked tooth was on full display. "I knew it would. You know my magic is on point."

"'Course it is," I answered right away, and this time I wasn't the only one. I made out Birdie, Cole, and my dad, along with Saxon, who'd sidled up next to Rhett and kept gazing up at him as if he were the best thing to ever bust through the pocket portal—not possibly the worst, as I was pegging him.

"I'd let you name the new drink," Sharmayne told me, "but you already named one today, and I can't go showin' favorites."

Which was a bald-faced lie; the woman had no

problems making her opinions known. She either liked you or she didn't, and you had no doubt which of the two it was.

"Besides," she added, "I already done named it."

We waited expectantly. It didn't matter that we were clearly in the middle of a crisis. Sharmayne was a woman who enjoyed her theatrics.

"Dragon Slayer."

Rhett growled loudly, and Saxon, who never smiled, grinned like a maniac, making the dwarf all but unrecognizable.

But I said, "That's a mighty fine name, Shar. And your concoction just saved my bee-hind."

Then, because I was tired of taking the scenic route when there were far too many problems to solve, I announced to everyone within hearing range, "I'm back to feelin' myself." A pronouncement that was at least one-third lie, two-thirds wishful thinking. "Time to focus on sheriff business. Who here can give me an update on Bobbie Sue?"

"Her brain's still a bit scrambled," Magnolia Roone called out, her husband the mayor notably absent from her side. The man was about as useful as a bent dog pecker. "But she's comin' round. She's taking a lie-down. I reckon she'll be back to her usual self once the sun comes up."

"Okay. Good. Lemme know if that changes." One problem more or less solved, only a few doozies to go. "Y'all can go back to your relaxin' now."

That was one order Denners never resisted. The chatter picked up immediately, and someone laughed somewhere in the back of the saloon, causing a chain reaction.

I relaxed another fraction. After the fire that had burned so viciously inside me, my whole body felt loose. Kiki was warm like a little heater, but I couldn't discount the possibility that her presence had helped me as much as whatever Sharmayne put in her Dragon Slayer cocktail.

I ran my hand along Tiger's side and looked up at Rhett. "Do I have to worry about you?"

"If you know what's good for you, you'll always worry about Rhett," Zeke chimed in.

I scowled at him. "*I mean*, does Rhett have his shifts and ... dragon magic ... or whatever you'd call it ... under control?"

"No," Zeke said at the exact same time that Rhett said, "Of course I'm in control."

Tiger leaned into my hand, so I scratched harder. "Clear as mud. Great. Just the kind of clarity I was needin'."

I pinned Zeke in a glare likely better pointed at

Rhett, but Rhett scrambled my mind even now that I could think more clearly. "Is Rhett gonna explode into a ball of fire or turn into a dragon and endanger others?"

"That depends on his mood," Zeke said.

Rhett thumped him on the back hard enough for Zeke to bounce forward.

"I'm not a danger to anyone else, if that's what you're asking," Rhett said, glaring at Cole. "But if people piss me off, I can be." His following smile was wicked.

"Good to know," I mumbled, sliding my drink back toward me and taking another sip. If I had to keep dealing with the likes of Rhett and Zeke—*and Cole*—I might need a few Dragon Slayers, and maybe a Sirens on the Rocks for good measure.

"Fine," I said, talking into my drink, peeved at the moment at everyone but Kiki and Tiger. Basically, anyone who could voice an opinion was on my shit side. "Everyone, try hard not to piss off the dragon shifter."

"Sage advice," Birdie said, tone mocking. I'd give her a firm hair tug later.

I drank some more, then busied myself petting Tiger again. "The dragon's egg. Where is it now? Is it safe?"

"Of course it's safe," Rhett snapped. "I'm a dragon shifter. I know how to take care of dragon eggs."

I attempted to breathe in patience and failed. This day had been too damn long already, and it wasn't even bedtime yet.

"*Where's the damn egg?*"

Rhett refused to meet my eyes. "Safe."

Zeke turned on him. "Tell me that doesn't mean what I think it means."

"I have no idea what you think it means, so I won't be telling you anything."

"You know you can't keep incubating it or it's going to hatch before we're ready!"

Since their arrival, Zeke had been remarkably steady tempered, all things considered. Even when he was pummeling Rhett, or wanting to pummel Rhett, or talking about beating the shit out of him, he hadn't lost his cool. Now, his nostrils flared and his pale face darkened with anger.

"Where else was I supposed to put it?" Rhett snarled. "I don't trust a single one of these people. Or creatures. Or whatever. You can't expect me to leave something as precious as a dragon's egg lying around for one of them to snatch it."

"We're not thieves, you raging idjit," Birdie said.

"And no one's gonna be appreciatin' you calling us that."

Of course, some of us Denners *were* thieves. But we didn't have to go owning up to that ahead of time.

"Till I know you, I don't know you," Rhett said.

"You're soundin' like a true Denner already," I grumbled. "So I take it you're still incubating this thing in your, you know, nether regions?"

This time it wasn't even my fault when I looked. His crotch was lined up with the table. I was as innocent as Kiki, snoozing on my lap.

But I looked away when I felt Cole's stare on me like the midday sun. Him, I refused to look at just then.

"The dragon's egg is safe," was all Rhett said before blatantly adjusting himself.

"That doesn't look too safe-like," my mom said. "Looks like you might squish that egg amid all that bulk."

"That's not all his bulk," Cole said. "He's got a dragon in there too."

"On to more pressing matters," I started.

Rhett adjusted himself once more, just to anger Cole, I figured. My eye was drawn to Rhett's groin by the movement, nothing else, I swear.

I huffed obnoxiously. Everything was spiraling out of control—yet again. "Okay ... so you don't know how long we have till the dragon hatches, especially with Rhett busy"—I circled my fingers in the air around his waist—"doin' Rhett. But what kind of dragon's gonna hatch whenever it does?"

"Yeah, Rhett," Zeke said, "what can we expect?"

For the first time, Rhett appeared uncomfortable. He hesitated. "I don't know."

"*You don't know?*" Zeke asked.

"No, I don't. But you don't either. And you're the one who took it in the first place."

"*You* brought this problem to us?" my mom accused Zeke.

He shifted his weight from one leg to the other, then ran a hand through his thick hair. "It's not like that."

"Then tell us," my dad said. "What's it like? Since y'all comin' here's endangered my daughter."

"I was saving the egg," Zeke said. "I was protecting it."

"Oh yeah, right," Rhett scoffed. "Because you always look out for us dragons."

Zeke was quiet for a few moments, his jaw clenching. Then he whipped around toward Rhett so fast he was a blur. "You know what, Rhett? I'm sick of your shit. I've been looking out for you for ages. And you know what? Now you're on your freaking own. You want to stuff a dragon's egg down in your balls though it's the stupidest thing you've probably ever done—and you and I both know that's saying something—then you deal with it when it hatches. I don't care what kind of dragon it is anymore, or if it's so rare it's the last one left of its kind. You want to do things your own way and blow up my house while you do it? Then you do you. I'm out."

And with that, Zeke whirled in another blur and zoomed out of the saloon so fast he left the double doors swinging in his wake.

"Whoa." Birdie whistled too for good measure. "What was all that about?"

"Nothing," Rhett grumbled.

"Sure didn't look like nothin' from where I'm sittin'," my dad said.

"Forget about it, okay?"

"No way in hell are we forgettin' about a thing," Birdie said. "This is the most fun I've had since Lo drank too many Moon Mixers and decided to compose an ode to Traitor's Den that lasted all night long. At least till she decided to go skinny dippin' in the river."

I added a few more hair tugs to her tab. She was *not* supposed to talk about that in front of my parents.

I pointedly refused to see if either of them were studying me. "Why does Zeke hate you?" I asked Rhett instead.

"Because we're brothers."

Even Kiki snorted half awake at *that* revelation.

"But…" Saxon began, then stopped to frown and rub at his long beard. "But you're a dragon shifter and he's a vamp."

Zeke was a vampire? Damn, how had I missed that? This day wasn't my finest.

"It's a long story," Rhett said.

"We've got time," I insisted, though I was beginning to wonder if I might drop from exhaustion before the dragon magic had the chance to wipe me out.

"Well, I'm not in the mood to tell it." And he stalked away. I watched his tight ass until it disappeared behind the doors, leaving them swinging again.

I tsked loudly. "Somebody go bring 'em back here. We're far from finished."

And then I finally dug out the note. The first

missive from the outside world since Traitor's Den had been founded twenty-three years ago.

"I'm not leavin' till we get answers." I slammed the note on the table while my dad and Cole walked out, Saxon on their heels.

"If we hear fightin', I'm gonna shoot first, ask no questions later. I've had enough of today." I patted Big Bertha for good measure, and I also patted Big Wilma for extra good measure. And then I drained the rest of my Dragon Slayer, doing my best to ignore the fact that I still couldn't use my other hand. It felt like I had my very own dragon incubating within the bite wounds.

"I'm mad as a box of frogs. If those two idjits know what's good for them, they won't mess with me anymore tonight."

Birdie sighed and wrangled a chair out from behind Tiger's flank, slipping her slim frame into it. "Lo, I don't mean to be the bearer of bad news, but I got the feelin' the night's only just getting started."

Then she turned, grabbed Ellie Mae's attention, and ordered us all drinks. When she noticed me watching her, she shrugged. "May as well make a night of it, dontcha think?"

Unfortunately, I had no better plan.

CHAPTER 15

*Double Trouble*

My first thought the next morning, even before I opened my eyes, was, *Damn, I must've forgotten to draw the curtains closed before I dragged my ass into bed last night.*

My face was hot; the room was too bright. I wrenched my eyes open to squint up at a beam of sunlight streaming in through high windows, then rolled my face out of its path—

Only to discover Kiki lying next to me, flat on her back, legs hanging heavily in the air, mouth open, with the tip of her pinkish-violet tongue peeking out of it. She was cute as a button and twice as cuddly.

*Awwww*, I thought to myself, unwilling to wake her by speaking aloud. Her soft, furry tummy was exposed, her chest rising and falling in the steady rhythm of deep sleep. One of her hind legs cycled a few times, and I couldn't help a wide smile. If only every creature to come through the portal could be as awesome as she was...

Memories of the night before were flooding in, reminding me how much trouble Rhett and Zeke had caused already—and they'd only been here a day.

Moving as little as possible so as not to jostle Kiki, I craned my neck to peek over the edge of the bed. Sure enough, there was Tiger, never one to leave me for long, especially not when I was in a vulnerable state, something I most certainly was, whether I liked it or not.

Unlike Kiki, he lay stretched out on his stomach, his head resting on his paws, ready to leap into motion at any moment despite the fact that he, too, was sleeping. His body was so large that it spanned the length of the circular bed.

There was only one place in Traitor's Den that had circular beds...

Which meant I was in one of the rooms on the second floor of Sharmayne's saloon, the ones Uncle Tucker's magic had devised as dens of illicit pleasure.

The whorehouse décor was pronounced. The drapes were a heavy scarlet velvet, same as the bedspread. Even the several lamps placed around the room, now off, were draped in the thick velvet and adorned with tassels.

Uncle Tucker. Nothing but classy...

Twinkling droplets dripped thickly from the high ceiling, stretching downward in slow motion until they dislodged, falling and then vanishing into thin air like shooting stars—or in the daytime, evanescent glimmers of a passing sun. That part was actually quite lovely, a detail that I didn't remember from before Kiki crossed the pocket portal to join us.

I was curled on my side on the gigantic bed, my injured hand stretched out in front of me with care, above Kiki's head and her new crown of branches and flowers. The tourniquet was gone, even though I didn't recall removing it, and the swelling along my arm had gone down. The bites on the back of my hand, however, looked just as worrisome as the night before. The row of punctures glowed an angry orange.

But I flexed my fingers a few times, my entire body relaxing at the movement. Things couldn't be all that bad if I could still use my hand without too much discomfort, right?

Last night, my dad and Cole had eventually returned, but without Rhett or Zeke. The newcomers had somehow disappeared—in the town that was entirely unfamiliar to them and that they couldn't escape.

Birdie had ordered a second round of drinks to soothe our general levels of frustration, and by the time the third round had rolled around, I no longer cared where either of the men were, so long as they weren't causing trouble I'd have to deal with later. By the fourth round, I was well and drunk.

We might be trapped in Traitor's Den, but we'd always survived it regardless. Dragon magic was new, as were dragon shifters and soon-to-be baby dragons. But there was nothing we Denners couldn't do when we put our minds to it.

After that final round, my memories were incomplete. Cole had perhaps headed back out to search for Rhett, likely to smash his face in, and my mom had insisted I should move as little as possible. I suspected my dad had carried me upstairs, content to leave me under Tiger's protection.

Stretching, I spotted my shorts, socks, and hat on a velvet chair in a corner, my boots beside it. The fact that my clothes were neatly folded meant my mom had been there too.

"Mmmm," I murmured softly as I took stock. I was still too hot, but I didn't feel as if I'd self-combust anymore. Great news. A subtle tingling circulated through my body, a reaction I assumed was caused by the dragon magic. Beside that and a brutal hangover, I could think straight again, though I wouldn't be ordering another Dragon Slayer anytime soon. I'd never had this intense of a hangover from Moon Mixers.

Just as I was pondering how important it really was to face another day of being Traitor's Den sheriff, or whether the more responsible thing was to sleep off this hangover, the bed shifted behind me.

I froze.

A moment later, an arm wrapped around my waist. Contented, sleepy murmurs whispered into the back of my neck before the chest pressed into my back rose and fell with deep, steady breaths.

I would've assumed this was Cole, who'd slipped into the room with me after I'd fallen asleep, only Cole smelled like leather, gunpowder, and cedar. And on nights when he'd been drinking, also like bourbon.

This man smelled like cool crisp nights that pebbled the skin, tangy metallic copper, and danger, though I wasn't certain what made me conjure up this last element. His arm was bare, corded with muscle and dusted with dark hair. The fingers were long, elegant, and smooth, not those of someone who'd worked all his adult life on a ranch as Cole had.

Just as I deduced that this was perhaps Zeke—though I had no idea why he'd be sleeping in bed with me—he readjusted, wrapping the entire length of his body against mine.

Even the hard, thick bits.

His lean, strong body spooned around mine, fitting my own form perfectly, making me ponder how well *every* part of him might fit me.

Breathing in his scent, feeling the cool comfort of his embrace and the way his body's desire for mine was insistent—undeniable—I was tempted to imagine what it would feel like to allow him to fill me. To simply go with the flow. To allow passion to lead me wherever it wished.

But I couldn't. Not when Cole wanted to marry me. Not when Cole loved me ... and I still loved him.

The man behind me pushed his hips against mine, his hand sliding across my bare waist to squeeze my flesh, his hard length positioned so that it would be all too easy to give into temptation.

To allow myself not to be responsible for once.

To be wild and free and not feel the weight of everyone else's wellbeing upon me.

He groaned behind me sleepily, seeming to begin

to rouse partially awake, resuming the grinding of his hips in earnest as he did so.

My body reacted to him without my permission, and before I could stop myself, I ground my hips back against his. I was in nothing more than my bikini underwear, and I could feel every thick inch of him pressing against me.

The dragon magic began to race inside me, my entire body flushing and heating like a flash fire. Or perhaps it had nothing to do with the foreign magic and everything to do with the electric sizzle that I felt from where our skin touched.

He hummed behind me, more loudly now, running his hand along the length of my side and nuzzling his lips against my neck. His cool, soft lips peppered languorous kisses along my flesh. My entire body heated to the next level.

My eyelids fluttered while I tilted my head to give him better access. His tongue drew a seductive line up toward the pulse point below my ear before nibbling on my earlobe.

I allowed a groan to slip out before remembering myself. Already distracted with need, I hazily noticed Kiki twitch in her slumber, and I thought I might have heard Tiger readjusting on the floor beside the bed.

Behind me, adept fingers slid along the edges of my panties, dipping beneath the lace band, drawing teasingly lower before rounding toward the front of my body, sliding lower still.

I arched my head back into his kisses, pressed my lower body into his. I could already tell I'd feel guilt over Cole later, but I couldn't stop myself. Didn't want to. As if halting would require inhuman effort. I wanted him more than I'd ever wanted anything else. *Anyone* else...

His tongue licked the length of my neck before kissing it, his hand sweeping across my tattered shirt and through one of the tears to cup my breast. When his nimble fingers grazed my nipple, I gasped and arched back into him, ready to give him everything he asked so long as he gave me more of what I craved.

It was as if I were an inexperienced virgin getting a taste of the pleasures of the flesh for the first time. As if what Cole and I'd shared for years had been nothing more than a warmup for the real thing.

Willing myself not to think for once, not to worry, I turned my head toward Zeke and allowed him to capture my mouth. His tongue was warm but not hot, and yet his kiss was hotter than anything I'd ever experienced before.

His fingers laced through my hair as he positioned his chest over mine, my body turning of its own volition to better face him, allowing him to cover me in one graceful move.

My injured arm lying limply out to the side, Kiki beside me, Tiger next to her ... I didn't care. I'd always believed myself honorable, respectful of others, and yet in that moment I didn't possess the strength to be that for Cole.

*Cole*, a part of me urged insistently. *I can't do this to Cole.*

But my body arched up into Zeke's despite my intentions. Our kiss deepened until I couldn't think at all, his tongue in a desperate dance with my own, his body throbbing in tune with mine.

*Stop*, I heard from somewhere deep inside me. *Cole*, that decent, honorable part of me tried again.

I almost sobbed from the resolve it required, but I wedged a hand between Zeke and me, flat against his chest.

He stilled, pulling back to search my eyes. No doubt which were wild and brimming with lust.

I couldn't speak. So I shook my head.

He pulled his face back farther to better study my own.

Whatever he saw there made him sit up, running a hand through hair dark as night, standing on end in all directions. With eyes so blue they nearly glowed, dark stubble, and lips a bright red, no man had a right to look that sexy.

But he did.

And I wanted him. A fact he no doubt knew.

Staring up at him, I breathed heavily. His breath came harder still.

His eyes blazed with a passion I hadn't understood how much I needed until just that moment.

And beyond him...

My eyes drifted over to the muscled body on the other side of the large bed.

Rhett was stretches of tanned, tattooed skin. Lines of ink wove across his upper body, forming, I now realized, a magnificent dragon. Waves of fire streamed from the creature's mouth, its wings wide, its eyes black. Its claws seemed to nearly rip from Rhett's skin.

And yet ... beneath the softness of sleep, the shifter appeared friendly, trustworthy even, his lips slightly parted as if he were innocent, when I knew he was not.

Dressed only in boxer briefs, they bulged with nothing more than him. The dragon's egg was nestled in the pillow beside his head, a guarded treasure.

My attention drifted back toward Zeke. He was staring at me, eating up every inch of my exposed skin. Desire continued to burn in his gaze ... to tent his boxers.

But his smile was tight. "Did you think I was him?" he asked softly in a voice thick with untold stories, raspy from unspent passion. He sighed and sank onto his knees. "It wouldn't be the first time."

Acutely aware now of everyone else in the room with us, I shifted onto my elbow, looking up at him. "No," I whispered. "I knew it was you. That wasn't the problem."

"Then what was?" He chuckled darkly. "Other than our audience."

"I don't know you. I don't trust you."

"Understandable. That will change."

"But that wasn't it."

He waited as I trailed my openly hungry gaze all over his mostly bare body. So much of my desire went into my inspection of him that he shivered. I studied every inch of him, even the parts of him that weren't exposed, *especially* those.

"I want you," I murmured. "Heaven knows that makes me crazier than a soup sandwich, but I do. There ain't no denyin' it."

He scooted closer, a hand trailing caresses across

my abdomen so gently they tickled. "Is it your arm, then? The dragon magic?"

"No. Though it'd make fine sense if it was that. I got one wheel down and the axle draggin'."

"You're more beautiful than any woman I've ever known."

I smiled at him. He was telling the truth, or at least he thought he was—that wasn't always the same thing.

I sighed. "It's Cole. I shouldn't have even done ... what I did with you. I just ... I couldn't help myself. I..." I trailed off.

"If you wanted me half as much as I feel the need for you, I fully understand. I barely managed to stop myself."

"But you did."

His eyes bore into mine. "I always will ... but I hope not to always have to."

I swallowed. *I hope for that too.* But that secret wish I didn't dare voice aloud. That would have felt like an even more important betrayal to Cole.

It was one thing for Birdie to help me realize Cole and I weren't meant for each other. It was quite another to go spreading around my decision before I told the man himself.

Cole deserved better than that.

Seemed like he deserved better than me, full stop.

"It's just," I whispered, "I've never felt that before. I didn't expect it to be like that with you. It felt ... it feels..." I searched for the right words and came up empty.

"Primal?" he suggested. "Right? *Necessary*? As important as breath and blood?"

I nodded slowly, reluctantly, though it wasn't exactly how I'd have put it.

That's when Tiger woke and stretched across the hardwood floor, groaning sleepily as he did.

That was also when Rhett's eyes popped open. He turned his head and zeroed in on me as if we'd been in the middle of a conversation.

He took in me in my advanced state of undress, then Zeke.

He scowled. "You taking what isn't yours, *brother*?" Rhett asked, and I got the distinct impression he wasn't referring to Cole.

I was in so much trouble, and the new day was only just getting started.

Searching for something to get me out of the hot water I was nearly boiling in, I blurted out the first thing I thought of: "The note. You never read the note last night. We need to see if you can read it."

I rose out of bed, careful of my arm, feeling the

heat of twin gazes on my behind with every move I made. That heat traveled across my stomach and through the holes in my shirt while I pulled my jean shorts back on, my shiny sheriff badge still looped into my belt.

I might feel like more woman than sheriff just then, but I could hide behind my duty to this town. I'd have to, before I lost any more control than I already had.

Spotting my twin six shooters on a night table, I buckled the holsters on.

"Well?" I said, and Kiki woke, smiling before she even opened her eyes. "We've got work to do and I'd rather not explain how the two of you ended up in bed with me."

I brought a hand to my waist, wishing for a shower, not daring to take one with either of them there. The odds of me not ending up fully naked with at least one of them weren't great. I wouldn't bet on me.

"How did ya come to sleep with me anyhow? I'm sure no one told you to do it."

Zeke shrugged. "We go where we belong."

Rhett didn't answer, but neither did he disagree.

*So much trouble.*

"Well, hurry up and get dressed. Someone'll

come lookin' for me before long, and I'd rather not have to answer questions about *this*." Especially as I didn't understand it yet.

Rhett stretched his arms over his head, exposing more lengths of dark inky coils. More dragon tattoos. Lines I could trace with my tongue...

"Aren't there better things we could do with our time?" he asked lazily, his voice a roll of seduction.

Hell yeah there were. Lots of them. Lots and lots and lots of them.

I slapped my hat on my head, slipped my feet in my boots—sans socks—and ran from the room.

And slammed into Birdie.

Who was standing right beside Cole.

## CHAPTER 16
## *When Bad Turns Worse*

My mind stammered and tied my tongue into a tight knot.

Birdie I wanted to see, so she'd saved me the effort of tracking her down. She alone could help me make sense of what in blazing hell was going on with the vampire and dragon shifter I had no business sleeping with. I refused to be a cheater. Between Letitia Lake and our fine mayor, there was enough infidelity going on in our town to sour my stomach if I let it.

But Cole ... I had to speak with Cole just as urgently, but not here and not now—and definitely not looking like I was sneaking away, double-dipped in sin.

"Um," I mumbled, off to a fantabulous start.

Birdie smiled broadly, though it felt forced; she probably already realized what had happened. She had an eerie knack for knowing when I was getting up to trouble.

"Loretta, we've been lookin' all over hell and high water for you. What in the dickens are you doin' here? Why aren't you home?" *Where you're supposed to be*, went unsaid, but I felt the recrimination just the same, my conscience working overtime already to plague me.

I glanced at Cole, who was studying me a bit too closely, making me starkly aware of my disheveled state. No doubt it was obvious that I was still dressed in yesterday's tattered clothes. But my sheriff badge was in place, along with my double six shooters. I straightened, forcing myself to remember that I had official business to attend to.

"I..." I started, stopped, then began anew. "I have no idea how I ended up here. You know what happened yesterday and how much I drank. If it wasn't either of you two who dragged me up here, then it must've been Momma and Daddy."

Realizing that I was just standing there like I'd been caught with my hand in the cookie jar, I hooked my good hand in my waistband and started walking, sockless feet feeling odd in my boots.

"Ya comin'?" I called back when they didn't immediately follow, wincing briefly at my choice of words. "I got work to do."

Birdie ran to catch up. "You sure you're up for it?"

"'Course I am. Duty calls."

Cole finally followed, the heels of his boots clicking along the wooden floor in tune with ours.

Birdie clasped my good arm to stop me. "Lo, you look like you hit ten miles o' bad road. No one'll blame you for takin' the day off for once."

I shook my head, refusing to look up at Cole now that he stood beside me. Usually, he'd be sliding his arm around me or kissing me good morning. He had to know something was up…

"I gotta figure this thing out before it's too late," I said. "We got a note to get read, an egg to, uh, situate, and I have a whole shit-ton of dragon magic inside me, where I'm pretty sure it don't belong."

They both hesitated.

"Come on already. I need to talk to both of y'all to boot. Let's get to my office."

"You sure?" Birdie asked. "Your hand looks like it's Butch's old chew toy."

I brought it up to study it, and even that small movement made it throb. She wasn't wrong. The puncture wounds had begun to ooze what I would've guessed was liquid lava if that weren't impossible.

I sighed. "That's why I gotta get to work." I set off walking again and they joined me, but when we reached the bottom of the stairs, Birdie asked, "Where are the two new guys? Fine as frog hair split four ways, them are. Mmm-mmmm."

I would have wished for Birdie to be subtle, but I'd given up on that ages ago.

"Oh!" I even widened my eyes, pretending to recall something. "Will the both of you please get me some coffee to go? I just remembered I gotta let Tiger out. You know, since he can't open doors yet." I chuckled nervously at my lame joke and tore up the stairs before one of them could offer to let Tiger out for me. Truly, I hobbled as if I'd been out for a day-long ride with Jo, but I did hobble as quickly as I could.

Pushing the door open without knocking, I about swung it open straight into Tiger's long body as he paced in front of it.

He chuffed at me in recrimination.

I ran my good hand along his back. "Sorry, T. I didn't forget about you. Promise. I just had to deal with somethin' afore I could come back for you."

He chuffed again, as if wary of believing me, but I never lied to Tiger. I didn't even bend the truth; there was no need to. I trusted him.

Besides, he couldn't tell my secrets, which helped immensely with the trust issue.

But then Zeke crossed the room and I forgot all about Tiger, my hand stilling on its way across his back.

The vampire had emerged from the adjoining bathroom, nothing but a small towel wrapped around his waist. Water droplets slunk down his chest, dipping over the ridges in his abdomen, and I found myself licking my lips before I became aware of myself.

His slow, sensuous smile told me he'd noticed.

His dark hair was wet, his eyes gleaming.

I wrenched my gaze away—

Only to discover that Rhett was still splayed out on the bed in nothing but his boxers.

All too aware that I could get lost for days in the dragon etched across his body, in the smooth, hard planes of his skin, I whipped my attention away again.

This time, it landed on a safe place. Kiki, sat placidly at the windowsill, turned to look at me. In slow, unhurried movements, she crossed the room, climbed up my legs, gentle with her claws, and looped her arms around my neck. Like an infant, she nuzzled her head into my shoulder, the branches crowning her head surprisingly soft against my neck.

She'd never hitched a ride with me before, but I brought my hand up to hold her closely against my chest.

Staring decidedly up at the ceiling where it was clear, I marveled at the tiny glowing orbs that dripped ever downward, until they disappeared; the effect was beautiful, and their magic would have been soothing if not for my present audience.

I told the two lick-worthy men: "Meet me at my office. And hurry. We got lots of shit to figure out, preferably before this dragon magic deep fries me and serves me pipin' hot on a fancy platter."

My socks rested on a chair, but I decided to abandon them. Stepping any farther into this room was dangerous.

Without making eye contact, I turned and followed Tiger out.

"Loretta!" Birdie hollered up the stairs, so I bustled down, my injured hand hanging limply at my side. Tiger walked alongside, protecting me from further injury.

"You're sweeter than sugar, Tiger, and twice as good for me."

Tiger chuffed—a multi-purpose sound in his arsenal. This time, he was pleased.

Hugging the glowing, regal koala in my arms, I didn't slow as I passed Birdie and Cole, leaving Cole to carry my coffee. Better to exit the building before Zeke or Rhett could come sauntering down in all their lust-inducing glory.

The moment I pushed outside, I sighed happily. "I've never been so relieved to have someone mess with my horse. Where's Jo?"

"Levi let her loose in the paddock with Bear," Cole said.

"Thank heavens." I ran a soothing hand along Kiki's back, when I was really the one in need of soothing.

I'd passed out and plumb forgotten about my horse, as if two lookers good for nothing more than distraction could be more important than my mare! A great horse was more valuable than a good man, every day, all day long. Anyone with a lick of sense knew that.

"Then I owe my daddy a big smack on the cheek for takin' care of her when I couldn't," and I set off toward my office.

The place was empty, though I suspected at least one of the men I'd woken with belonged inside its cells.

"Just give me a sec to clean up some," I told them as Birdie held the door open for Tiger, waiting for him to relieve himself.

"Take more than a sec," Birdie said. "You need it."

I smiled tightly at her, doing my best to ignore the way Cole trailed my every movement but said nothing.

"Thanks, Bird. You're a real peach."

"For you, anytime," she said, letting Tiger in as I slipped into the bathroom.

I'd never had reason to shower there before, but I had plenty now. Kiki climbed off me to rest on the edge of the sink, next to my pile of clothes, hat, badge, and revolvers.

As I made quick work of washing, she watched, and had she not looked as if she'd wake-and-baked a heaping bowl of Jujayjay, I might've been discomfited. But she gazed at me like some magnanimous god who'd seen it all, so I did my best to pretend it was normal to bathe under the watchful eye of a shimmering, iridescent koala who put the *magical* in magical creatures for all time. I also attempted to ignore how the bite on my hand sizzled continually as the water rained down on it.

By the time I emerged in the same clothes as before—couldn't be helped—but squeaky clean, Birdie and Cole were sitting close to each other, next to my desk. Tiger stood at attention, cat eyes trained on Zeke and Rhett.

Zeke leaned lazily against a wall, one foot kicked back onto it, and Rhett, hair also wet, straddled a chair. They tracked my every move like hunters.

I knew all too well whom they considered their prey...

Claiming the chair behind my desk, I settled Kiki on my lap and kicked up my feet.

"Glad y'all could make it so fast. Clearly you know how to hustle when the hustlin's good."

Immediately after, I caught my error and plowed on before Cole or Birdie could ask questions to which I didn't have the kind of answers I wanted to share aloud.

"The note," I said while I dug it out of my pocket. It was a bit worse for the wear, crumpled and torn only a wee bit, but every unintelligible rune was still legible.

Unwilling to hand it over to the man I didn't trust, I beckoned Rhett over to the desk.

"Can ya read it?"

He carried his chair over, positioned it beside my desk, and resumed straddling it. The spokes of the seat back framed his loins like a picture frame.

As sheriff, I studied the scenario, concluding quickly that he either had left the dragon's egg in the room, or he had enough bulk to hide it.

*Lawd, this man was more trouble than a forest fire.*

Refusing to check on who'd seen me doing my job of looking for the egg, I snapped, "Well? Can you read it or not? It's time to fish or cut bait."

"Oh, I can read it all right."

That got Zeke to saunter over, leaning over Rhett to study the note. Zeke's sleeves were rolled up, and his forearm muscles popped as he pressed them into my desk.

I shot a quick look at Birdie, hoping for some sympathy. How was a woman supposed to focus with all these beautiful cowboys waltzing around?

But Birdie was busy admiring too.

And Cole was, once more, watching me.

I groaned but swallowed my frustration. I was gonna lose my mind worrying about all this nonsense on top of dragons and dragon magic.

"Well?" I asked. "We're trading daylight for dark."

"I hear what you're saying," Rhett said, "but I have no idea what you mean half the time."

"That'll change real fast," Birdie said. "Uncle Tucker's magic goes changin' ya up." She tapped her temple. "You'll start thinkin' and soundin' like a good ol' cowboy in no time. Good on you, you already look like a good 'un. Both of you."

Birdie ... being unhelpful in the midst of being helpful, as was her usual way.

"What my girlfriend means," Cole said, "is that you'd better hurry it up. We've all got far better things to do, and I still need to whoop your ass for all that you did yesterday."

And Cole didn't know the half of it...

*Good gravy.*

"You can read it, right?" Zeke asked Rhett.

He paused. "I can."

"*And...?*" I was gonna strangle the man before the day was over. Then we'd have a total of three dead Denners. Maybe I'd even take Tiger over to piss on his grave after the man was good and buried.

"And it's not good," Rhett said.

I plopped my hat on my desk and leaned my head

back, talking up at the ceiling. "Someone grant me patience before I kill a somewhat innocent man."

"He's definitely *not* innocent," Cole said.

I didn't dare agree.

Rhett looked up at Zeke.

"That bad?" Zeke asked.

"Worse."

The dragon magic inside me seemed to intensify, though it might have just been my own pulse kicking up a notch. I didn't need bad, and I so didn't need *worse*.

"You're new, so you might not know this about me yet, but I'm a rip-the-bandage-off-fast-and-clean kinda gal. So let me have it."

"You're gonna die."

Birdie gasped, Tiger chuffed, and Kiki smiled happily—I was thinking I needed some of whatever she was smoking, pronto.

Cole, however, blurted out: "I kissed Birdie"—like it was a squeaky fart he couldn't hold in any longer.

Annnnnnd *worse* somehow got *worse-er*.

## CHAPTER 17
## *Dragon Shifters Perform*

Like a skipping record, my thoughts kept looping around the same points, over and again while I petted Kiki robotically. I was gonna maybe die—*maybe*, because I didn't trust Rhett enough to fully believe anything he said. And Cole kissed Birdie. *My boyfriend kissed my best friend.*

Cole and Birdie had shot through the pocket portal with their families when I was thirteen, a few months apart from each other. We'd been near inseparable ever since.

Yes, I realized that the fact that Rhett thought I was going to die was far more pressing, but I couldn't seem to help the direction of my emotions.

"My boyfriend of eight long years, the only

man I've ever been with and whom I love, kissed my best friend, whom I also love," I said, my voice flat.

"Did you even hear what *I* said?" Rhett asked.

I waved him away, too busy glaring at my two friends across the desk from me to care about my mortality just then. That would surely change soon enough, but—

"I can't believe you two."

Of course, I had kissed Zeke—more like, I'd let Zeke kiss me—but Cole and Birdie had kissed first. They were on their way to find me when I was bolting from the bed I unintentionally shared with the two hottest men in town. It wasn't like *my* actions landed me in bed with them, all of us half naked. I'd passed out from the dragon magic and Sharmayne's booze, which I consumed in mass quantities to soothe the burn of the bite, and woken to the most tempting circumstances possibly known to any woman alive.

But I'd resisted them—more or less, though I was gonna go with *more* right then.

"No wonder the town's called Traitor's Den. Uncle Tucker wasn't as far off as we all like to think he was."

"I'm so sorry, Lo," Birdie said. "I never meant for

it to happen this way, and it's not really like all that. We didn't exactly *kiss* kiss."

"We did kiss," Cole blurted, face flushed from what I assumed was his guilty conscience. His stinking, steaming heap o' guilt.

Birdie tsked. "Yes, obviously we kissed, but that's not what I meant."

I smiled dangerously at the best friend I'd never contemplated having to do without—before now. "What *did* you mean then?"

"Just that we didn't set out to kiss. It sorta just ... happened, ya know? It wasn't like we were sneakin' 'round behind your back. It happened and we were lookin' for you to tell you right away. We weren't gonna lie to you 'bout it or nothin'."

"So you were lookin' for me, not because you were worried about me, not 'cause this idjit here"—I jerked my head in Rhett's direction, including Zeke too at the end, just 'cause everything had gone to shit in a smelly handbasket since they'd *both* shown up—"says I shouldn't move much 'cause this magic inside me's dangerous? Says it's gonna kill me? But 'cause you two were out neckin' while I was doin' my best to survive? *To live*?"

I'd been working to survive the burning power inside me *and* the two men I associated with it, not an easy task. Not when they looked the way they had no right to look and acted how they acted.

Cole's eyes were wide and alarmed. "We weren't neckin'. It was just a quick peck." He paused. "Or maybe a few..."

"A 'quick peck' on the cheek?" I smiled again, each time feeling more heat bubbling inside me, every time knowing my smiles grew more grim and more menacing.

"No," Cole admitted heavily. "Full on sugar on the lips."

"We didn't know Rhett thought you were dyin' then," Birdie inserted quickly.

"He told me yesterday I might die. And you saw me last night. I passed out like a ninny 'cause of how much it all hurts!"

My eyes started smarting, so I figured that was enough of that. I was no ninny.

Birdie shifted forward, leaning her elbows on my desk. I sat back, staring down at Kiki curled across my lap, trying to shift my focus to how magnificent she was.

"Of course I—we—were and are worried 'bout you," Birdie said. "Come on, you know what it's like. We've been friends forever. You know I'd never betray you or nothin'. After our little chat on the way over here—"

I whipped my head up to glare at her so fast that she shrank back in her seat.

*Oh, so now you're gonna betray my confidence too?* my look said, plainer than words.

She sighed. "I just thought that after we talked, about you know what—which I'm not gonna say, don't you worry—that, I dunno, you wouldn't be angry?"

Ah, Birdie ... the best, best friend and the worst, all at once.

Cole wasn't stupid, and he was studying me now like he was putting all the pieces of Birdie's not-so-subtle puzzle together.

Tiger circled my desk, nudged his large head between their seats, and nipped at each of them in turn.

Birdie squeaked, and Cole jerked his head back so fast that it hit the wood of his chair back. I hoped that hurt.

"Don't be such babies," I said uncharitably, not in the mood to forgive them just yet, though I already knew I would. We'd been through too much together to let a few kisses ruin what we'd built. "Tiger isn't gonna bite y'all."

Tiger growled loudly as if to say, *Hell yeah I'll bite the crap out of you both if you dare hurt my Loretta.*

Birdie and Cole flinched, their faces scrunched up in a mirror of anguish.

Now Tiger ... *he* was the most loyal friend a girl could have.

"Thanks for always havin' my back, T. You're the best."

And then I looked pointedly from Birdie to Cole and back again.

Tiger nodded, chuffed, then sauntered back over to my side, long sleek muscles rippling with every step. He didn't need a magical glow or a crown blooming with real flowers to be as extraordinary as Kiki. When he drew near, I stopped petting Kiki to scratch his ears.

I didn't dare move my bitten hand from where it lay limply across my lap. With how volatile I felt, I didn't want to do a single thing to accelerate the dragon magic pumping inside me with every beat of my heart.

Staring boldly into Cole's gaze, I told him, "I accidentally kissed Zeke this morning. *After* you'd already made out with Birdie, by the way."

"Actually," Zeke said in a roll of seduction that had my body contracting all over, "I kissed you."

Rhett swiveled in his seat to face Zeke. "You did *what*?"

Zeke scoffed. "You're only angry because I kissed her first."

"Damn right I am."

But I was too busy watching Cole, determined not to look away from him, even as his face heated and his jaw waggled back and forth. He was angry. Worse, he was hurt.

I sighed loudly, sadly, as if the room weren't filled with a bunch of busybodies. "Look, Cole. I love you. I truly do. With so much of my heart."

He opened his mouth.

"Wait. Please. I didn't want to do this with an audience, but we need to settle this so we can move on and figure out what to do about ... well, everything else. Before I crack into a million pieces, and by the way I'm feelin', it's a real possibility."

I took a deep breath and kept going. "You're everything I could ever want in a man. You're kind, thoughtful, respectful, and funny. You're handsome and awesome and just seein' you makes me smile most days. But..."

"But," he repeated mournfully.

"But we're not meant for each other. Not like that anyhow. And I think you must've known it for a while now."

Immediately, he began shaking his head so fervently that his shaggy hair bounced all over the place. "No, Lo, *no*. We *are* meant for each other. This was just a mistake, on both of our parts. We're both wound so tight you couldn't drive a toothpick up our butts with a sledgehammer. This will all pass and you'll be fine. *We*'ll be fine, I promise."

"You can't promise that, Cole. I love you so much, but I just don't think we're meant to tie the knot. Maybe all we were ever meant to be is great friends."

"No. No way. Un-uh. I'd rather be in hell with a broken back than lose you."

"Sounds like it's not up to you, buddy," Rhett said.

Cole whipped around in his chair so fast that I thought he'd knock it over with his ass still in it. "I'm not your buddy, and you'd better back the hell-balls off my girl before I make you."

"From what I'm hearing, she's not your girl."

Cole started to rise from his chair.

"Enough! We're burnin' sunlight, and I'd

mightily like to make it through to nightfall. Can we all focus now?"

I used my *sheriff look* to get them all to eventually nod their agreement.

"Good. Now ... tell us more about what the note says, Rhett."

The door swung open and my mom and dad rushed in. Their attention zeroed in on me as if they were bloodhounds tracking my trail.

"Ohmylawd, honey," my mom said. "You look like you been rode hard n' put away wet." She grimaced a little. "But still beautiful, of course."

I chuckled, because life was over-the-top crazy, and it seemed like high time I embrace the ever-lovin' goodness out of it.

"How you feelin' today, sweetheart?" she asked. "And do ya have any news for us?"

"Take a seat. We're about to find out."

While my parents drew up chairs, Rhett studied the note again.

"So these are definitely dragon runes, an ancient language used by the sorcerers among dragon shifters."

"There are dragon shifters who are *sorcerers* too?" Birdie asked. "Why do I not like the sound of that?"

"Because ... what's to like?" I asked.

"Dragons can read the language," Rhett went on. "But they can't write it, for obvious reasons." He held up a hand, wiggling his fingers. "So this has to've come from a dragon shifter."

"And there aren't many of them left," Zeke said. "There aren't many dragons left either, actually."

"No." Rhett smiled sadly. "Such amazing creatures, and no, there aren't that many left. They've been hunted to near extinction and forced to retreat to the Nightguard Mountains. A secret I'd never share, except that you can't tell anyone outside of the town."

"And where are these mountains?" my dad asked.

"Does it matter now?"

"I suppose not."

"They're so high up and isolated that they're hidden from common knowledge. Their location is a sworn secret of all dragon shifters. We are the protectors of the remaining dragons."

I arched my brows at Rhett. "You're a protector?" I deadpanned. "You don't act like one."

"Not only is he a protector," Zeke said, "but he's *the* protector."

From the admiration in Zeke's voice, I would

have never guessed he'd burst through the portal trying to pummel Rhett to death.

"Without him leading them," Zeke continued, "I don't know what will happen to the dragons now."

"They'll be fine," Rhett said gruffly. "The others are plenty competent."

"But they aren't you."

Rhett grunted. "Nothing I can do about that now. If you hadn't been trying to steal the egg back, fighting me over it, I never would've ended up jumping through the portal."

"And you could've trusted me when I told you I wasn't going to harm it. That I'd only stolen it from the vampire masters of Shèng Shān Monastery to eventually give to you. That I was helping you protect the dragons."

"Then you should've given it to me when I asked for it, instead of waiting for me to take it."

"And *you* should've *trusted* me, for flying farts' sake." Zeke winced at the unwelcome imagery. Yeah, Uncle Tucker's F-bomb denial was no fun, I was feeling him on that.

"I'm your damn brother, Rhett," Zeke insisted. "Was it too much to ask for you to trust me?"

"We're not true brothers, and you know it."

Zeke didn't say a word to that, but I could feel his heart squeeze from where I sat.

Rhett must have felt it too; he turned to look up at him. "That's not what I meant."

"You said what you meant." And Zeke took a step back from him, opening up a divide wider than a gully. "So what does the damn note say already?" His tone was cold enough to freeze the balls off a pool table.

"It says that if we don't return the dragon's egg to the Nightguard Mountains by the full moon, the dragon bite will finish what it started. Clearly, they don't realize I have the egg now instead of vamps, or they wouldn't be worried."

I swallowed thickly. "What does 'finish what it started' mean exactly?"

Rhett placed a hand on my desktop as if he were reaching for me, to comfort me, I thought, though it seemed highly out of character. "It means that dragon magic is continually oozing into you through the bite on your hand. It further means that there's a final, lethal dose waiting to enter your body if we should refuse to meet their demands."

"And dragons don't play around any more than dragon shifters do," Zeke said. "At least when it comes to performing their duties anyhow."

Rhett looked back at him; Zeke refused to meet his eyes.

"And no one or nothin' can leave Traitor's Den," Birdie whispered. My parents looked too shocked to say anything at all for a few moments.

Then, my mom asked, "How long do we have? Do we know if the moon cycle in here aligns with the moon cycle out there?"

No answer, because none of us knew.

"For all we know, time could be passing faster out there than it is in here," Cole said in an anguished wobble.

"Well, then," I said, uselessly. I didn't know what else to say.

What else was there to say?

My twenty-third birthday was only a few weeks away.

And I still might not make it.

CHAPTER 18

*The Heart of Traitor's Den*

My dad was in his usual seat at the head of the dining table, and I plunked down heavily beside him. Birdie, Cole, Rhett, and Zeke occupied the remaining chairs, leaving only my mom's spot open. No one dared touch it.

Kiki had resumed her position in my lap, appearing to do nothing but sleep as she curled up, but despite her inactivity, comfort oozed from her violet fur. She alone was helping to calm my nerves.

Tiger spread out on the floor beside me, but though his head rested on his paws, his whiskers and tail twitched, his muscles spasmed occasionally, and he purred softly—and menacingly—as if he were busy wishing the imminent threat to my life were something he could bite the head clean off of.

If only it were that easy...

Even Jolene and Bear huddled outside the large kitchen window behind the sink, listening in, and Butch whined from where he'd plopped on the floor beside my dad. The old hound dog had never been the smartest, but he was as loyal as they came. He looked from my dad to my mom and then to me, trying to figure out why the air in the kitchen in my parents' house was tenser than a balloon at a porcupine party.

No one said a thing while my mom slammed around mixing bowls and pots, whipping every ingredient as if her life depended on it, even when I was pretty sure most of the recipes didn't call for any kind of whipping. She'd even closed the fridge so hard that it sputtered in protest for a few moments before settling into uncomfortable silence along with the rest of us.

After my mom had insisted we move our meeting from my office to her kitchen, refusing to heed my protests, Birdie had offered to help her prepare the meal. My mother's response had been a sharp "There's only room for one cook in my kitchen"—snapped like a rubber band. None of us had dared utter a word since.

Even the soup she was making churned on the stovetop, clanging against the sides of the pot as if wishing to escape the scene.

When my dad started breathing heavily, like a bear about to charge, as if he couldn't contain the turmoil that was surely rumbling inside him any longer, my mom stomped over to the pantry, grabbed an entire pot of honey, and set it down in front of him, patting him on the back as if he were a child.

Now my dad was licking a honey dipper and I was beginning to wonder if impatience would kill me long before the dragon magic racing through me had a chance to.

"I can't take it anymore," I said, before I knew I had decided to speak.

"Oh, thank my lucky hat," Birdie said. "I'm not made for not talkin' like this."

I ignored her, thankful she'd chosen to sit beside me so I didn't have to stare into her traitorous best-friend face.

"Momma, I don't think we've got time for a nice sit-down meal."

When my mom stopped moving entirely, her

shoulders rising with her back to me, I hastily added, "Though it's a kind enough thought to wanna make one for us all."

I waited a beat to make sure she wasn't actually about to explode. Her body seemed to vibrate, too ramrod straight. "We gotta get to figurin' out if there's a way to save me."

My mom whirled to face me, crossing her arms in front of her chest, getting flour on her shirt despite her apron. With the way her eyes swirled with visible desperation, I didn't think she'd have noticed if she dumped a whole pound of flour on herself.

Her lips trembled. "*We came here* to figure out what to do. There's no ifs about it. Sure as rosy shit, we're gonna save you, that we are."

My dad nodded while he slurped up honey, his mouth sticky beneath nostrils that flared in furious determination.

I smiled at them, though I suspected the gesture didn't come off as encouraging as I intended. The dragon magic flared inside me, back to burning my insides like I was busy slamming back Sharmayne's Dragon Slayers, one after another.

"I don't see how you keepin' busier than a one-armed monkey with two peckers is gonna solve the problem, Momma. It's not all on you. I'm the sheriff, 'member? I got this. You don't have to solve my problems for me anymore. I—"

"Don't you sass me, Loretta Maybelle. I'd rather be beaten with a sack of wet catfish than stand around and do nothin' but watch you get taken over by this *magic*." She spit out the word, usually revered in Traitor's Den, like it was fouler than pig shit. "You look like a strong fart in a whirlwind could blow you away, and your daddy and I aren't 'bout to let that happen. Not on our watch."

"I'm not your little girl anymore. I don't need you to fix everything for me. I'm fully capable—"

"Honey," my mom said, "I couldn't be prouder of the woman you've become. You're stronger and smarter than most, and you got a good heart, carin' for others like, and in my book that's more important than any of that other stuff. I'd bet my favorite boots on you bein' a better shot than Declan James, no matter how many times he toots his own horn. You keep the trouble-makin' idjits in this town in line when our fine mayor can't keep it in his pants long enough to notice. *You* are the heart of this town."

She paused. "But that don't mean you gotta do everythin' yourself. Not when it's your own life on the line, and not when you got all of us on your side ready to help you fight your battles."

I slid my feet aimlessly on the floor. I did feel like day-old shit warmed over ... but did everyone have to notice?

Adjusting my hat on my head and patting Big Bertha and Big Wilma, I did whatever I could to avoid looking into all the stares pinned on me from across the table.

"I think better when I cook," my mom stated. "You know that. 'Fore the lasagna hits the table, we're gonna have this problem solved."

I looked up at her. "How?"

"I know you've felt alone a lot of your life, bein' the only one in town not to have magic and all, but honey, y'aren't. And now you got these two strappin' young men lookin' to fight for you too."

I purposefully avoided studying the "two strapping young men" after my mom bared my greatest vulnerability, serving it up like it was the first dish in the maybe-six-course meal she was preparing.

"Wait," Zeke said, speaking for the first time since he'd sauntered through the threshold to my childhood home. "Loretta doesn't have magic? I thought everyone in town had magic."

"Everyone has to have magic to see the portal to

get into Traitor's Den," Cole said, his voice an unsteady mixture of anger and defeat. "But once you're already in it, the town won't kick you out if you don't have magic. There's no leavin' town after you land here. You're stuck, through and through. You come up on the invisible boundary that circles the town? It just pushes ya back like it's a real wall. But it won't boot ya out, never does."

If what Cole said was true—and it's what we'd all believed for as long as we'd been here—then I was as screwed as Letitia Lake when she scored.

"Then how...?" Rhett started, trailing off, his full pink lips scrunched up in consideration.

Birdie leaned onto the table, picking at her cuticles without looking at them. "Loretta was born here. She was the only one to pop out already here for a long while, till little Frances came along."

"And was Frances born with magic?" Zeke asked.

I felt my cheeks flush, and for once I didn't think it was from the killer magic looping mercilessly inside me.

"Yup, she's got magic for sure," Birdie told the two newcomers with a fond chuckle. "She's been shockin' the livin' daylights out of her parents since she was wee."

"Literally," Cole added, though little Frances

didn't actually shock anything *out* of her parents, who walked around with their hair standing on end, continually looking like they'd plugged directly into the magic that ran this town.

"You don't have magic," Zeke said. "I can't believe it."

Since there was only one person he could be addressing, I forced my gaze up to meet his. Smiling tightly, I nodded. "Believe it all right. I'm pretty damn sure, trust me."

Short of jumping off a cliff to see if I might sprout wings and fly, I'd done just about everything else I could think of to attempt to trigger my magic.

Birdie and Cole had been witnesses to many of my experiments, alternately cheering and egging me on. And now I wasn't in the mood to even look at them...

"How's this possible?" Rhett asked my parents while my mom turned to stir the contents of a pot and check on her lasagna as it cooked in the oven.

"You're a shifter," he told my dad. "And—"

My mom whipped back around, flicked a hand in the air, and caused the vase with flowers in the middle of the table to hover. It floated over to Rhett's head, then upended, water streaming out—but not the flowers.

"That's for disrespectin' my daughter when you first got to town." Then my mom directed the vase back over to her, filled it up at the sink, and lowered it back to the table.

"I'm a witch," my mom added without need, resuming some stirring.

"Fair enough." Rhett removed his hat and flicked water off his shirt, onto the floor.

While Rhett got up to empty the rim of his hat out the open window, and Cole grinned like my mom had just given him an early birthday present, Zeke asked, "How's it possible for Loretta not to have magic? She should be a shifter or a witch, one of them for sure."

Grimacing, I took off my own hat, tossing my hair in an attempt to cool my head. Every part of me was burning. I tossed my favorite black Stetson on the table.

"Let me cut to the chase so we don't waste time we ain't got to be wastin'. I'm supposed to have magic but I don't. I'm sure as sure gets. At first, we thought I might get my powers in the course of puberty like some others do. But nah, I didn't. It sucks harder than Letitia tryin' to win a stubborn man over. But 'tis what 'tis."

A soft tongue slid over the festering bite marks

on the back of my hand, and I glanced down to see Kiki licking away, each move of her head causing the pink-tinged blooms crowning her head to sway. I rubbed at her back with my other hand, and she hummed happily.

At least one of us was content despite front row tickets to the shitshow.

"I need to find Tucker so he and I can have some words," my dad suddenly announced, though the sentiment was far from new. "When I see him again, I'm punchin' him straight in the nose, and I hope it breaks and heals all crooked like."

Zeke, and Rhett, back in his seat, though still wet, arched their brows in identical fashion, looking like brothers for once despite their many differences.

I sighed, resigned to airing more dirty laundry, figuring I'd tell the story quicker than my parents, who tended to reminisce about the early days when they were falling in love, no matter what the circumstances.

"Daddy's brother Tucker was in love with Momma. Then she and my daddy met, and it was love at first sight."

"That it was," my mom commented fondly while she checked on rising dough.

"It wasn't like Tucker had a claim on her," my

dad grumbled. "They weren't married or anythin' when I met her."

"Though they were *engaged* to be married," I interjected; it had to be said.

My dad released the honey dipper into the pot with a clank as he sat back in his chair, his shoulders bunching up. "Colette wouldn't've agreed to marry him for a second if he hadn't kept me from her."

"And by that," I said, "he means that my Uncle Tucker didn't tell him he had a girlfriend. Or a fiancée."

"I just happened to stop by to see him 'bout somethin', and I spotted the most beautiful woman I'd ever seen, sittin' out in the garden, the sun shinin' on her face—"

*Like she was a flower ready to bloom*, I completed in my mind; I'd heard this version of their story many times before. Even Birdie was probably able to recite my dad's words by now, though I had no desire to look her way to check. I could feel her eyes on me, willing me to stop avoiding her.

I cut in before my parents could gather steam. "Long story short: my momma called off the engagement, Tucker got pissed, called my daddy a traitor—"

My dad scowled. "And created this town as a

punishment for *me*. He's a powerful mage, that he is. But he'd never used his magic to punish me afore. He'd always done right."

My mom leaned against the kitchen island, wiping her hands on her apron with a sad yet still dreamy smile on her face. "When Tucker opened the portal, we had no idea what it meant. He didn't give us a second to figure it out before he shoved Levi through it. It was closin' real quick, and I just knew I'd never see the man I loved if I didn't follow him through." She released her apron, coming over to kiss my dad on the head, resting her hands on his shoulders. "So I did."

My dad spread his hand over hers. "Last thing either of us heard from the outside world was my brother cursing my name."

My mom looked over at me. "We didn't know then that Loretta was already growing inside me." Resolve washed the memories from her face. "Tucker's already taken your freedom from you, honey. Ain't no way in hell or heaven that I'm gonna stand by and let what he did steal anythin' more from you."

"It's not been all bad," I said to relieve some of the guilt my parents had been carrying for as long as I could remember. "Traitor's Den has a certain kind of charm."

Birdie snorted. "Charm isn't the word I'd use."

"Too right, Birdie," my mom said. "This town is about as ripe and varied as a fruit bowl."

My mom moved to slap both palms flat on the table, making Tiger jerk his head up, the horses neigh, and Kiki's tongue pause in its soothing trajectory across my skin.

"But for better or worse, it's home. And I believe it's gonna give us the way to save you."

"Why?" I asked. "Why do you believe that? It's not like this town has a magic of its own. It's all whatever Uncle Tucker wanted, and he didn't even know what a Western frontier town was really supposed to be like. It's just some big hodgepodge of hokey and random stuff. The magic of this place is *his* magic."

"I don't think that's true anymore, honey. I think the Den's growin' right along with us."

I slid my chair back, trying to carve out space when my insides felt like they were starting to suffocate me. "Is that really what you think? Or is that just what you want to be true?"

"Both. But it doesn't matter. We're savin' you one way or another. I won't accept anythin' else."

And with how fierce my mom looked right then, I thought I might just be able to believe her.

"All right. So what do I do?" I gently moved Kiki away from my hand as I prepared to stand.

"*You* are gonna sit right there and not move. Remember what Rhett said."

"Yeah, yeah." *The more I move, the faster the dragon magic spreads.* "But I gotta do somethin'. I'll go crazy just sittin' on my ass."

"You can help by puttin' that sharp mind to use," my dad said, "while makin' sure you give us all the time you can to figure this out. Eat your momma's cookin'. Build strength."

He cocked his head, studying me. "Or maybe just focus on not passin' out."

I bit my lip, unable to argue. I did feel like a stiff wind could blow me away faster than it could a tumbleweed.

"Well, we could ask all the mages in town to try to summon the portal again," I suggested, trailing off at the end. "The magical creatures too, for good measure. We have a few days before the moon goes full. And maybe this time we'll actually be able to get at least a note to stay on the other side instead of rushin' back to bonk Ashton Blu on the noggin'."

"They've tried before, many times," Birdie

pointed out. "The portal's never opened for any of us."

"Then they'll try again," my mom said, bustling to the window. "Jo, Bear, go fetch Bluebell for me, will ya?"

The horses tossed their heads and whinnied.

"And I need you to be faster than a hot knife through butter."

The stallion and my mare spun and sprinted off as if my mom had pulled a trigger. The sound of their pounding hooves made the dipper rattle against the ceramic of the honey pot.

"Son," my dad said, making me glance up, wondering to whom he was talking. He rarely called Cole "son."

Rhett's brow was furrowed.

"You look like you got an idea stewin' there."

"I just might."

Zeke turned to face the dragon shifter. "You can't be thinking what I think you're thinking."

"And if I am?"

"It'll kill her!"

"It might."

I groaned, shoved my hat back on my head, and shifted Kiki onto my seat while I stood.

"Sweetie, don't," my mom said, rushing toward me, hands out.

"I need air or I'm gonna explode early."

Birdie slid her chair back. "Don't worry, Missus Ray. I'll keep an eye on her."

I looked over my shoulder. "No. You won't. I'll take Tiger with me though."

Tiger rose from his stomach, his shrewd amber eyes pinned on me with as much determination as a soldier heading into battle.

Cradling my thumping, pulsing arm, I walked slowly from the kitchen, out the door, and around to my little studio apartment in the back.

I told myself my measured pace was so no one would worry unnecessarily about me. But that was a lie as big as any I'd ever told myself.

The moment I closed the door to my place behind me, I crumpled like I had no bones in my body and just focused on breathing.

I knew I didn't have long before I'd need to head back. I wasn't quite sure why I'd stalked off in the first place. There was no time for introspection. The full moon was coming all too soon, and I intended on living to see my birthday.

But for a second or two, I'd allow myself to mourn the truth of the matter: despite all my efforts, despite all the help I'd receive, I might not succeed. It might not matter how many good intentions my parents or friends had, Uncle Tucker's magic had never yielded before.

Traitor's Den was a town built on magic—and vengeance.

It was a prison with no escape.

Tiger nuzzled his head against my shoulder. I lowered my face to his fur and thought of nothing but the comfort he offered freely.

The knock on my door arrived before I was ready...

## CHAPTER 19
## *Save-Our-Fine-Sheriff Mission*

The last thirty hours passed in a rush of frantic communal despair, which had an unexpected effect on me. The more Denners around me freaked out, the calmer I became. Strange, I knew, but I was grateful for the odd reaction. If I had to face my death, then I'd rather do so with a deranged smile on my face than reveal my regret at leaving so much undone.

None of our harebrained schemes to solve my imminently lethal problem had worked.

Bluebell hovered next to my ear, her wings flapping so quickly that they buzzed and blurred like a hummingbird's, only the sight of her no longer made me smile. Since my mom had called on her for help, she'd self-appointed herself commander of the Save

Our Fine Sheriff Mission, a result that my mother had never intended, proven by the way she narrowed her eyes to perilous slits every time they alighted on the thimble-sized fairy. Which was often, given that Bluebell hadn't left my side long enough for me to kick the urge to swat at her, and my mom hovered around me at regular intervals, fussing at my hair, my clothes, anything she could adjust or straighten just to feel she was doing something to help.

I sat in a rickety wooden chair off to the side of Portal Platform. I'd protested, of course, but my parents had insisted, and I didn't have the heart to refuse them, not when my dad couldn't stop accidentally growling. He'd already scared the crap out of Hank Henry, who'd been as skittish as my mare since then. Jolene, as even-keeled as any horse I'd ever met, stomped her hooves, tossed her head, and snorted with a wild look in her eye. She understood what was going on as much as anybody else; she'd taken to running off to burn through some frustration before returning to stand nearby, squealing loudly behind me.

There was nothing I could do to soothe any of them but sink into my dubious throne and watch over the catalog of attempts to open the portal—the many *failed* attempts.

Once, the bell had rung, and even I'd jumped in a rush of excitement. But it had only been Ace Steele, who thought he'd seen the portal open from the viewing stand above. What he'd actually observed was Rhett losing his cool, igniting the dreaded dragon note into flame in the palm of his hand. The paper had burned quickly, and when it was over, every single Denner present at the platform had glared up at Ace Steele. Lucky for him, he hadn't noticed, proclaiming in an official tone that the portal had disappeared just as quickly as it had opened.

But the man, though blind as a bat, wasn't hard of hearing. I doubted he'd missed the many grumbled insults hurled his way.

I sank farther down into my chair, silently grateful for its support. With the way the dragon magic was burning through me, I wasn't sure I could stand on my own anymore, and certainly not for long.

Sweat dripped along the sides of my face, between my breasts, and down the curve of my back. I'd stopped wasting the energy to sop it up hours ago. The day was hot as most were in the desert that barely changed seasons—thanks for that, Uncle Tucker—but the sun was kissing the horizon, and twilight was ushering in. With it, a drop in temperature would cool the parched earth. I knew this to be the case, but I couldn't feel the relief.

I was burning up from the inside out.

My hand rested on Tiger. He'd barely left my side, chuffing so regularly that it sounded like an agitated purr. The shifter, usually far warmer than I was, felt cool in comparison to the heat running through the palm of my hand.

The burn was inescapable. Just as it seemed my fate might be...

"Ow," I yelped at a sudden biting pain on my earlobe. A blur of translucent wings zoomed out of view.

With a groan of wood beneath me, I swiveled to pin the buzzing fairy in my sights. "I'm gonna jerk you bald, Bluebell. Why the hell'd ya pinch me? I swear to holy basil, if you don't stop messin' with me I'll tear your arm off and beat you to death with the bloody stump!"

Bluebell smirked at me. "As if you have the strength for that... You're as spright-lookin' as a stretch of bad road."

"I won't deny that, but think of this. If I do end up dyin', I'll haunt you till the end of your days. Do you really wanna be messin' with me now that I might be nearing death's door?"

That got the fairy to purse her lips in a troubled scowl.

*Score.* I hadn't even known if the bothersome magical creature believed in an afterlife.

Bluebell, who'd shot through the portal with a head of periwinkle-blue hair and a gauzy skirt and crop-top to match, crossed her diminutive arms over her equally diminutive chest. "Well, then you'd best stop starin' off into space like you got all the time in the world to figure yourself out. News flash, Loretta: ya don't."

Tiger chuffed extra loudly, and Jolene whinnied in support.

"Do ya really think I don't know that?" I asked, the heat raging inside me bubbling up into my words. "What do you want me to do? I've even tried summoning the portal myself, and I don't even have magic!"

Bluebell landed on my leg, but Tiger snapped at her, giving me my first chuckle in what felt like ages.

The fairy jetted back into the air to hover in front of my face. Her tiny nostrils flared and she tossed her bright bob in irritation. "Nasty tiger."

Tiger nipped at her again. This time, he let his enormous teeth all but scrape her behind.

She squeaked. "Dammit, Tiger. Stop carryin' on like we got nothin' better to do. I'm tryin' to help our girl here."

"Coulda fooled me," I muttered.

"Besides," Bluebell said, clearly not finished with Tiger yet, "I'll have you know that though I look sweet and pretty as one a Emmaline's meringues, if you bite me, I'll be bitter as a stink bug. I'll make sure of it. So for your sake as much as mine, back the flyin' toot off." Then she snarled.

I imagined that, to her small ears, she sounded vicious. To me, she sounded like a door hinge in need of oiling.

"How exactly are you tryin' to help me?" I asked. "Unless you mean by driving me crazy, and if that's the case, you needn't bother. I'm pretty sure I'm half there all on my own already."

"Holy balls, Loretta. Are you blind as Ace *and* stupid as Lonnie too?"

I huffed and looked away, spotting Rhett, Zeke, Cole, and my parents in a heated argument just out of ear shot. Jony, my mom's best friend, was tugging on her arm, trying to restrain her.

"Are you listenin' to me?" Bluebell snapped.

With an obnoxious sigh, I studied her. She'd ditched the matching clothes the very day she arrived in Traitor's Den, claiming that her magic hadn't allowed her to wear anything but periwinkle blue in the outside world.

Today, she was dressed in daisy-duke shorts that all but showed her miniature yet pleasantly round ass cheeks; a pink-and-red checkered shirt, tied up to reveal her flat mid-section; and the cutest little red cowboy boots, small enough that I might wear them as earrings.

"I'm doing my darnedest to help you get your head out of your ass, darlin', not annoy you."

"Coulda fooled me." As my attention began to wander back over to the argument I couldn't hear, she flew forward and kicked me on the cheekbone with the tip of said red pointy boots. Twice.

"Ow, you little..." I swatted at her with my good hand but missed as she zoomed out of the way. I didn't rise from my seat, concerned I'd land on my face.

"Stop feelin' sorry for yourself and get to doin' what you do best."

"Which is?" Menace rode each of my words, gritty as if I were the dwarf Saxon Silver. "And I'm *not* feeling sorry for myself."

Though maybe I was—just a little.

"You solve problems, set things right, and do it all in time to get sloshy over at Sharmayne's after dinner. It's what you *do*. You've done it for us Denners a thousand times over. Now all you gotta do is step up for yourself."

Sighing in defeat, I slouched back into my chair, grateful I no longer had to kill the fairy. I didn't have the oomph to do it, and I wasn't a fan of idle threats.

"BB, I'm tryin' all right. I been tryin' since I first found out I was in trouble. We've had near on every Denner there is come through here to try their hand at opening the portal. We've even thrown notes at the empty air just in case that might do something. I've even *meditated*, for flute's sake, and I ain't never had use for sittin' still and overthinking things in my entire life. I've seen myself pushin' the dragon magic out of me like it's a stiff turd. Even my momma's tried to send it away, and Jony too. The two a them've had every witch and wizard in town doing their spells over me.

"I've guzzled lots more of Sharmayne's concoctions, and she made 'em with the purpose of ridding me of this magic I got, and you know her abilities are on point. Saxon's forged charms for me that he said should work"—I raised my good arm to jangle the silver bracelet he made me, dripping with charms, one in the shape of a dragon head—"and even Brewster's been racing around, butt cheeks speedin' here and there, while he's ... well, I guess I'm not sure what all the pygmy troll's been doin', but he swears it shoulda worked. Kiki's been lyin' in my lap more often than not, glowin' like she's been, and Doc Holloway's made me drink every nasty thing she can think of."

I winced at the memory of the bitter contents of each vial she forced me to ingest.

"Emmaline even cooked up some sweets for me with her magic baked right in them, sayin' there was at least a shot they'd help. They did nothin' but please my sweet tooth. Even Durwood Toole came by to see if he could help, and you know the gnome hardly ever shows his bushy face in the more frequented parts of town."

I met eyes with the fairy. "I'm stucker than a duck in a dry pond. Not even Rhett knows what to do to save me, and he's a *dragon shifter*. Supposedly some highfalutin dragon *protector*. If anyone should know how to deal with this problem I got, seems like he should. But he and Zeke've been circlin' around me like they're long-tailed cats in a room full a rocking chairs. None of us know what to do. It's gotten so that my dad's chargin' the air where the portal always appears, as if that would do a damn bit of good. Solvin' this particular problem's as slippery as tryin' to nail a gelatin mold to a tree trunk."

Tiger sat in front of my legs, lowering his heavy head to my lap, and making Bluebell buzz out of the way to hover by my ear.

"So you're back to feelin' sorry for yourself, I see," she said.

I swallowed hard, trying to keep my temper from flaring since it wouldn't do me any good. "I am *not* feeling sorry for myself. I'm just tellin' you the truth as it is, you bloody pest. If I could think of a single thing to do to save myself, don't you think I woulda by now?"

"You're *smart*, Loretta. You know this town and its rules better than anybody. If somebody's got a chance at making a prison break, it's you. You've been here from the start. You were born *inside* this magic. You're part of Tucker's world whether he planned it or not."

I tilted my head to one side, wondering if that could be true. "I don't have magic..." I started, turning her words around in my mind. "You think Uncle Tucker's magic could still be a part of me, even if I don't have any of my own."

"Loretta, darlin', there's one thing I know good and certain: there are no set rules for magic, least not any that stick every single time. You don't got magic of your own, fine. But you live inside what amounts to a magical bubble. You don't think that's had some effect on you all these years?"

She paused, her beady eyes intent. "At the start, it was just you, Colette, and Levi. You were a baby when they already had their magic developed. Don't you think there's a chance you coulda absorbed more of Tucker's juice than he bargained for? He didn't even know you were gonna be part of the picture. He didn't account for you."

"That part's true as arrows shot with a steady hand." Excitement mingled with the dragon magic raging through my body, making me feel lightheaded, and I didn't think it was Sharmayne's latest batch of experimental spell-infused booze I'd downed an hour before.

"And now I have dragon magic mixing all up with it," I said, all too ready to believe that Bluebell might be on to something.

Tiger whined and looked up at me, seeming to ask if he had reason to hope I'd survive the next full moon.

"That's right," Bluebell said. "You likely got

some a Tucker's magic brewin' in ya. You got dragon magic, and that kinda magic is as powerful as it gets. And you might still have some of your pappy's magic too, or your momma's. It shoulda shown up by now, one way or another. Maybe it's there and you just don't know it yet."

When my mom sent Jolene and Bear to fetch Bluebell, it had been because she was the most effective gossip in town. With her fast little wings, she darted here and there, whispering the latest into people's ears, choosing the Denners most likely to help spread whatever juicy tidbit faster than a bee-stung stallion.

None of us had expected her to do much more than recruit every Denner with a chance of contributing to head over to Portal Platform.

Nibbling at my bottom lip while I ran my hand across Tiger's head, I stared at the festering bite mark on the back of my other hand. Tiny lava pits roiled within each of the wounds. There was no sign that they intended to heal; they were incontrovertible proof that I had some sort of magic inside me.

"Maybe you're right," I whispered, overcome with awe, as Bluebell's points assembled in my mind for further examination. At her self-satisfied hum, I regretted my admission. Her ego was already ten times bigger than she was.

Then shouts drew our attention to the right of the platform. My dad, mom, Jony, and Cole tried to restrain Rhett, but he charged past them as if he were an enraged bull, shoving Cole hard. Cole landed on his butt—and Cole was no lightweight. He tussled with the best of them, never one to keep his nose clean for long when around the thrill of a fight.

But Zeke, whom I figured would have been the first to attempt to hold back his brother, helped keep the others from reaching him.

With a sharp look, Rhett reached into his pants and dug around, drawing my eye to the bulge I couldn't ignore even if I wanted to. He emerged with the dragon's egg.

After saying something to Zeke, he placed the egg in the vampire's open hand more gently than his demeanor suggested him capable of, shook Cole off another time, sidestepped my dad when he barreled at him—

And ran toward me.

I squeaked in surprise—possibly also in alarm—before I became aware of myself.

Tiger turned toward Rhett, bared his teeth, and growled.

But Rhett kept coming, and he hadn't been all that far away to begin with.

When he skidded to a stop in front of Tiger, Zeke bodychecked my dad while holding the egg overhead.

"Everybody, freaking stop right this second," Zeke yelled.

Every Denner who heard him turned to look.

"I will *not* let him hurt my baby girl," my dad said, moving past Zeke, who turned and snagged my dad by the shirt.

My dad roared a bear roar, but Zeke held fast, waiting until he stopped before saying, "It's our last chance to save her."

"The moon's not full yet," my mom said, stalking toward us with fury illuminating her eyes as if they were lit by Uncle Tucker's magic itself.

Rhett answered her, but watched Tiger, whose snarl was vicious enough that anyone in their right mind would heed it.

"The moon cycles might not be in sync. We've exhausted all our options. It's now or never. If y'all interfere, we might be too late."

To my surprise, Tiger tipped his head to one side, telling Rhett he was listening.

Rhett crouched down, putting his face in front of Tiger's rows of impressive teeth.

From behind, Zeke pressed a hand to Cole's chest, holding him back. Birdie popped up beside them, tugging on Cole's arm.

"I'd never hurt her," Rhett told Tiger. "I promise you, this is the only way I can think of. You have to let me act before it's too late."

Tiger chuffed as if to say, *I'll be watchin' you, motherfluter*, then ... stepped out of the way.

My protector was purposefully exposing me to whatever Rhett wanted to do that had my parents in a frenzy.

My mouth dropped open as Rhett charged me. Bluebell zipped out of the way.

In the next instant, his arms wrapped around me tighter than a vise.

I attempted to swallow my whimpers as the fire inside consumed me.

All I could see behind my pinched-shut eyes was the orange of flames.

CHAPTER 20

*From Embers to Ashes*

For once in my life, I wished I were a ninny. I could have been like Emmaline Bay, who swished around town in her long skirts, saying "I do declare" with little prompting, in a voice sweet as sugar, and overall doing her best to convey the impression that she needed a man to prop her up —an impression that heartily failed since she was highly competent in her confectionary kitchen. Or I could've been like Ellie Mae Sanders, who fainted at the slightest cut that oozed blood, a marked disadvantage when she waited tables at Sharmayne's Den, where fights broke out on the regular.

But *no*. I'd spent all my life working to prove that I could contribute to this town as much as anyone with magic, which was *everyone else*. I'd weeded out any sign of weakness—at least insofar as anyone else might notice.

I wanted to pass out, really I did. But I'd ferreted out that kind of nonsense ages ago.

So instead I felt every sensation that whipped around in my body, pummeling everywhere at once as if I'd internalized a brutal thunderstorm, with hail the size of pomegranates. Or a volcanic eruption, more like, where the lava spread and overcame all parts of my being.

Eyes shut tightly, I focused only on getting through to the end of whatever Rhett had done to me, all the while hoping, wishing, *praying* that I'd lose consciousness and wake up again when it was all over. I was especially focused on coming through this to the other side, a conclusion I wasn't at all certain of at the moment.

Every little bit of me burned—even my toenails and the fine hairs lining my nostrils. My eyeballs felt like they might burst as inevitably as overripe grapes, and just as messily. My heart thumped erratically in my chest, seemingly never sticking the right rhythm for long enough to put me at ease.

Each breath was a fait accompli as my lungs squeezed and clenched and made me feel like I was on the bed of Sandy Bottom River, having to fight to kick to the surface of the turbulent waters for each and every inhale.

I couldn't decide whether I was standing, sitting, or lying down. I couldn't even figure out if Rhett's arms still banded around me, or if the sensation of his hold merely lingered.

Perspiration soaked my skin worse than in the dog days of summer. I wanted desperately to strip free of my soaked clothing.

Bright lights swirled and pulsed inside my vision like a host of fireflies, flying here and there, but never straying far enough.

Buzzing like that of a hundred insects consumed my hearing, managing to further isolate me from my external circumstances. I could be plopped in the middle of town, naked as a jaybird for every Denner to ogle, and I'd have no idea.

A pop loud like a firecracker set my ears to ringing at a higher pitch. I wanted to swat at my ears to soothe them, though of course that'd do no good.

But then the ringing settled, and it was as if it had dispatched the horde of insects swarming the inside of my head. My surroundings were muffled and faint, but *I could hear again*.

People were fighting. Tempers were rising. Groggily, I attempted to identify the voices. It took a while, longer than was reasonable considering there were only so many Denners stuck in this town with me.

As if still on the bed of Sandy Bottom River, muffled, I heard my mom growl as if she were the bear shifter of the family instead of my dad. She'd never done that before that I could remember; I only knew it was her because of the accusation she spit out next.

"I'm gonna skin you alive, Rhett Steed. I don't care that you got all those fancy tattoos all over ya. It's gonna be a bloody waste of ink. You mighta killed my baby girl!"

While I was busy regretting her insistence on referring to me as *baby* anything, she growled again, and this time the menace reached me more clearly.

"I didn't kill her," Rhett said, his words nearly as much of a growl. "I'm trying to *save* her."

"You've got a shit way a showin' it," my mom squeaked, and choked on her words. "Just ... just look at her."

There was a long pause during which I presumed my mom and Rhett, and whoever else might be standing around with them, turned to study my sweat-soaked delirious self. I wondered if I looked as badly as I felt.

"She might be dyin'. My baby might really be dying," my mom added. "She looks like death warmed over. She's sweatin' like a hog marked for dinner."

*Yup. Guess I do look about as good as I feel.*

"She hasn't woken up since you grabbed on to her. That was hours ago. *Hours*, asshole."

"We *told you* not to touch her," my dad said in a deep rumble that suggested he was two wrong steps away from shifting into his black bear form whether anybody wanted it or not.

"I don't care what either of you think," Rhett snapped, proving he had no idea how protective my parents were of their only child, or to what extremes they'd go to defend me. Also, that he was a dumbass *and* an idjit.

Even Tiger snarled at him from somewhere nearby.

"I'm connected to her just as much as any of you are," the town idjit went on.

"Excuse me?" my mom breathed. Had I been able to move, I would have been backpedaling away from her as fast as I could. "You think *you're* as connected to her as *we* are? *As I am?*"

"Yes."

"Oh, so you *grew her* inside you for near on a

year and then pushed a baby the size of a prize-winnin' butternut squash out of your tight butthole?"

An uncomfortable pause. "I didn't falutin' think so, you can o' rotten turds," said my mother.

*Wow.* That was ... unpleasant imagery.

"I'm obviously a man," Rhett said, and even in my half-baked state I couldn't help but wholeheartedly agree. That he was.

All man. All scrumptious.

He chuckled warmly. "See?"

Someone tsked, then I heard Zeke. "Look, Mister and Missus Ray, ignore him. He never learned to be civilized. But what he's getting at is true. Filling her up with his dragon magic was the only chance at saving her with the time we have left."

*Filling me up?* I thought with an immature smile that didn't show on my face. Only after did I register the much more important part: *dragon magic.*

Rhett's dragon magic? That's what he'd done? Like I needed more of the liquid fire that was trying its darnedest to eat me up from the inside?

"Yes, dragon magic," Zeke said.

"She already had dragon magic burning through her," Cole said. "That was the whole problem."

*Thank you, Cole.*

"Not *his* kind of dragon magic."

*Hmm-hmmm.*

Another chuckle. From Rhett, I thought.

Zeke went on: "The dragon magic injected into her through the bite was aggressive, with a lethal intent. Rhett pulsed the magic of his ... nature, I suppose I could say, into her. It will give her a certain resilience against the lethal magic." A long pause during which hope was busy building happily inside me. "At least, that's our theory. We hope it'll work. It's possible it won't. This has never been done before, not like this."

"That's for damn sure," Rhett inserted.

What little hope I'd managed to gather skittered away as fast as a mole who'd caught the scent of a trap.

"*More* dragon magic isn't the answer," Cole said. "Dragon magic is the whole problem."

"It was the best option after we'd exhausted all other ones," Zeke said to a grunt of agreement from Rhett.

"We hadn't exhausted our options," Cole retorted. "The moon is only just now about to rise, and—"

"And what?" Zeke pressed, as aggressive and as volatile as Rhett. "Another round of you all flaunting around on that wobbly platform, trying to get a portal to show up that isn't coming? Chanting and flicking your fingers at the empty space? Or were you going to launch a few more notes into thin air, hoping they'd vanish and somehow magically get delivered to the dragon who's ready to kill Loretta? For all we know, the moon's already up on the other side of this town. Dragon magic is certainly powerful enough to cross dimensions. Haven't you seen sufficient proof of that?"

"Well, if all that's the case, it wasn't your place to decide," Cole snapped. "Loretta is our responsibility."

I bristled without the real strength to get behind my irritation. I was no frail maiden in need of hand-holding.

"Damn right, it wasn't their place," my dad said, sixty-percent bear.

"That's where you're all wrong, and where, for once, my brother is right," Zeke said, a dangerous edge tinging his words. *"She belongs with us.* It's our job to protect her now."

A new wave of heat swarmed through my body, making me groan. This time, the rush didn't necessarily hurt.

"She knows it too," Zeke added.

"Like hell she does," Cole shouted, and I guessed he was either cocking his fist back to let a punch fly, or about to set some of his magic to crackling in his hands. Battle magic.

"Cole," Birdie warned, sounding like she was probably placing a hand on him to try to calm him.

"She's *my girl*. She belongs with me, not either of you two buffoons."

"Just because you want something to be true doesn't make it so." Zeke's statement was free of the fresh wave of emotion that had begun swirling in the well of my stomach.

"I'll curse you—" Cole started.

"*You will not.*" Zeke's words vibrated with a power I hadn't felt from him before. "If we did something that gave you the impression that we're some kind of pushovers here to kowtow and kiss ass, you can go ahead and get that nonsensical notion out of your heads. Rhett is *the* dragon protector. He's at the top of a ladder that reaches so far up it kisses the Nightguard Mountains. In the supernatural community, he's so high up that his existence is secret. Only those in the know have any idea he even roams the world, protecting dragons and, ultimately, all of us. No one wants dragons feeling threatened and raining hellfire on the world to defend themselves and their young."

"And my *brother*," Rhett chimed in, "is no ordinary vampire. If what I did doesn't save her, he's going next."

Snarls, growls, and a jumble of insults and threats from my mother, tempered by some attempts at moderation from Birdie, pounded through my head. I winced—or, I thought I might have.

"You know I got your back, Colette." *Jony*. My mom's best friend. "Let's kick some pretty tight asses." A crack that sounded like knuckles.

Then Tiger roared, and I couldn't hear a thing for several seconds after. That could've been from the volume of his warning, or it could've just been me. I had no way to know.

"You see?" Rhett said. "Tiger understands. He gets what we're saying."

Tiger was on *their* side? I didn't think I understood a thing anymore...

"Shut up. All y'all, stuff a dirty sock in it," Bluebell interrupted, sounding close by. "The moon's comin' up right now. We'll find out if what Rhett did worked soon enough."

"Zeke, be ready," Rhett said. "If she starts

convulsing or shooting fire from her eyes or mouth, she's gonna need your strength to survive it."

My eyes popped open at the thought of shooting fire from *anywhere*.

I stared straight up into twin full moons. They were too close. Too consuming.

The moon was claiming me for sure.

Then violet, silvery eyelids drooped lazily over the twin orbs ... before rising again.

*Oh. Not moons. Kiki?*

Was she standing on my chest?

She started humming ... or perhaps that was me. Or maybe it was the dragon magic—times two—inside me.

I blinked up into Kiki's glowing eyes until heat and flame and fire and everything hellish burst inside me so that all I could do was scream.

Then darkness finally crowded me, lulling me toward it, more tempting than a tall glass of cold water after a day trekking through the desert, trying to kill me from thirst.

The fire could rage all it wanted now. Nothing could be worse than this.

I'd either wake or I'd die, but at least there'd be no more liquid fire sweeping through my veins, bubbling under my skin until it surely blistered all over.

Encasing my lungs, my heart, my head in its unsurvivable heat.

*You'll be finer than a monsoon rainstorm, don't you worry your pretty lil' self. There are always rainbows, my girl.*

I opened my eyes a final time to blink up at Kiki. I thought it'd been her in that odd lackadaisical voice I'd never heard before.

A reassuring smile cracked her furry face.

I smiled back with a wheezing surge of strength —a final sputter—glad I could go out doing something nice.

I succumbed to the dragon magic pumping through me from the bite on the back of my hand.

To Rhett's version of the magic, apparently potent enough to make him some sort of alpha to dragon shifters.

To the full moon, which hadn't delayed despite my many silent pleas.

To Uncle Tucker's curse that made me a prisoner of my own life. That trapped me in a town filled with others possessed with magic, making me a freak among freaks—entirely too ordinary.

To a destiny that wasn't mine to control. To a fate I had no more chances to wield.

I faded away into nothing.

My final thought was to hope that, deep within, I'd cultivated the strength to rise from the dying embers.

Because I sure as shit was burning until there'd be nothing left but ashes.

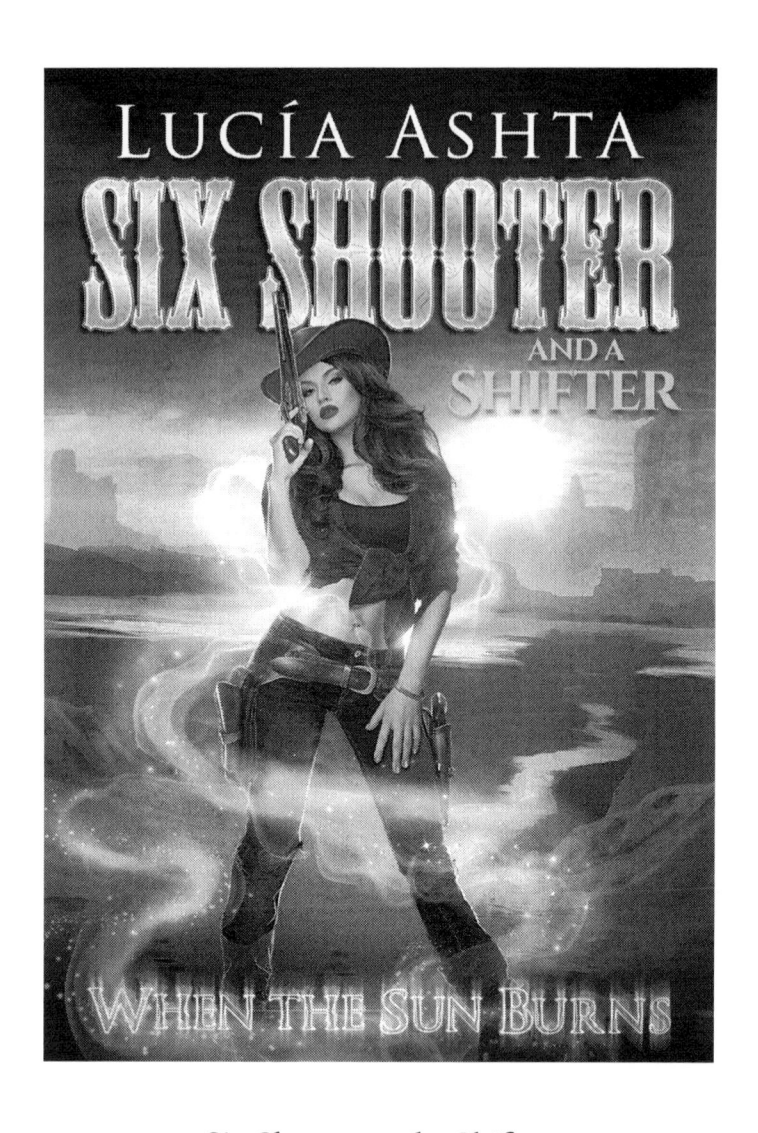

**Six Shooter and a Shifter**
**Book Two**
*When the Sun Burns*

Continue the explosive adventure with Loretta, Rhett, and Zeke in **WHEN THE SUN BURNS**, the next book in the Six Shooter and a Shifter series.

# Books by Lucía Ashta

## ~ FANTASY & PARANORMAL BOOKS ~

## WITCHING WORLD UNIVERSE

### Warrior Monks
*Return of the Viper*
(coming soon)

### Highlands Pack
*Immortal Howl*
(coming soon)

### Magical Enforcers
*Voice of Treason*
(coming soon)

**Magical Dragons Academy**
*Fae Rider*
(coming soon)

**Six Shooter and a Shifter**
*When the Moon Shines*
*When the Sun Burns*
*When the Lightning Strikes*
*When the Dust Settles*

**Rocky Mountain Pack**
*Wolf Bonds*
*Wolf Lies*
*Wolf Honor*
*Wolf Destinies*

**Smoky Mountain Pack**
*Forged Wolf*
*Beta Wolf*
*Blood Wolf*

**Witches of Gales Haven**
*Perfect Pending*
*Magical Mayhem*
*Charmed Caper*

# BOOKS BY LUCÍA ASHTA

*Smexy Shenanigans*
*Homecoming Hijinks*
*Pesky Potions*

## Magical Creatures Academy
*Night Shifter*
*Lion Shifter*
*Mage Shifter*
*Power Streak*
*Power Pendant*
*Power Shifter*
*Power Strike*

## Sirangel
*Siren Magic*
*Angel Magic*
*Fusion Magic*

## Magical Arts Academy
*First Spell*
*Winged Pursuit*
*Unexpected Agents*
*Improbable Ally*
*Questionable Rescue*
*Sorcerers' Web*

*Ghostly Return*
*Transformations*
*Castle's Curse*
*Spirited Escape*
*Dragon's Fury*
*Magic Ignites*
*Powers Unleashed*

## Witching World
*Magic Awakens*
*The Five-Petal Knot*
*The Merqueen*
*The Ginger Cat*
*The Scarlet Dragon*
*Spirit of the Spell*
*Mermagic*

## Light Warriors
*Beyond Sedona*
*Beyond Prophecy*
*Beyond Amber*
*Beyond Arnaka*

# PLANET ORIGINS UNIVERSE

## Dragon Force

*Invisible Born*
*Invisible Bound*
*Invisible Rider*

### Planet Origins
*Planet Origins*
*Original Elements*
*Holographic Princess*
*Purple Worlds*
*Mowab Rider*
*Planet Sand*
*Holographic Convergence*

## OTHER WORLDS

### Supernatural Bounty Hunter
(co-authored with Leia Stone)
*Magic Bite*
*Magic Sight*
*Magic Touch*

## STANDALONES

*Huntress of the Unseen*
*A Betrayal of Time*
*Whispers of Pachamama*

BOOKS BY LUCÍA ASHTA

*Daughter of the Wind*
*The Unkillable Killer*
*Immortalium*

## ~ **ROMANCE BOOKS** ~

*Remembering Him*
*A Betrayal of Time*

# Acknowledgments

I'd write no matter what, because telling stories is a passion, but the following people make creating worlds (and life) a joy. I'm eternally grateful for the support of my beloved, James, my mother, Elsa, and my three daughters, Catia, Sonia, and Nadia. They've always believed in me, even before I published a single word. They help me see the magic in the world around me, and more importantly, within.

I'm thankful for every single one of you who've reached out to tell me that one of my stories touched you in one way or another, made you laugh or cry, or kept you up long past your bedtime. You've given me additional reason to keep writing.

My thanks also go to my beta reader team, advance reader team, and reader group. Your constant enthusiasm for my books makes every moment spent on my stories all that much more rewarding.

# About the Author

Lucía Ashta is the Amazon top 20 bestselling author of young adult, new adult, and adult fantasy and paranormal fiction, including the series *Smoky Mountain Pack*, *Witches of Gales Haven*, *Magical Creatures Academy*, *Witching World*, *Dragon Force*, and *Supernatural Bounty Hunter*.

She is also the author of contemporary romance books.

When Lucía isn't writing, she's reading, painting,

or adventuring. Magical fantasy is her favorite, but the romance and quirky characters are what keep her hooked on books.

A former attorney and architect, she's an Argentinian-American author who lives in North Carolina's Smoky Mountains with her family. She published her first story (about an unusual Cockatoo) at the age of eight, and she's been at it ever since.

*Sign up for Lucía's newsletter:*
https://www.subscribepage.com/LuciaAshta

*Hang out with her:*
https://www.facebook.com/groups/LuciaAshta

*Connect with her online:*
LuciaAshta.com
AuthorLuciaAshta@gmail.com

facebook.com/authorluciaashta
bookbub.com/authors/lucia-ashta
amazon.com/author/luciaashta
instagram.com/luciaashta

Printed in Great Britain
by Amazon